CONFESSIONS
THE PARIS MYSTERIES

JAMES PATTERSON is one of the best-known and biggest-selling writers of all time. Since winning the Edgar™ Award for Best First Novel with *The Thomas Berryman Number*, his books have sold in excess of 300 million copies worldwide and he has been the most borrowed author in UK libraries for the past eight years in a row. He is the author of some of the most popular series of the past two decades – the Alex Cross, Women's Murder Club, Detective Michael Bennett and Private novels – and he has written many other number one bestsellers including romance novels and stand-alone thrillers. He lives in Florida with his wife and son.

James is passionate about encouraging children to read. Inspired by his own son who was a reluctant reader, he also writes a range of books specifically for young readers. James is a founding partner of Booktrust's Children's Reading Fund in the UK.

CONFESSIONS
THE PARIS MYSTERIES

JAMES PATTERSON
AND MAXINE PAETRO

1 3 5 7 9 10 8 6 4 2

Young Arrow
20 Vauxhall Bridge Road
London SW1V 2SA

Young Arrow is part of the Penguin Random House group of companies
whose addresses can be found at global.penguinrandomhouse.com.

 Penguin
Random House
UK

First published by Young Arrow in 2014
First published in paperback by Young Arrow in 2015

www.randomhouse.co.uk

A CIP catalogue record for this book is
available from the British Library.

ISBN 9780099568254

Printed and bound by CPI Group (UK) Ltd, Croydon, CR0 4YY

 Penguin Random House is committed to a sustainable future
for our business, our readers and our planet. This book is
made from Forest Stewardship Council® certified paper

CONFESSIONS
THE PARIS
MYSTERIES

1

THE
BEST
OF TIMES.
THE
WORST
OF TIMES.

1

Hello, friend.

I'm writing to you from Paris on a stunning day that is way beyond anything I could have imagined. I thought I was prepared for this, but I was *wrong*.

I remembered how I endured months of a forced and hellish separation from my boyfriend, James Rampling, when I didn't know if he was alive or dead. How my mind was wiped of nearly every memory of our time together, until I doubted his entire existence. So now, as I stood in front of the astounding Musée du Louvre, scanning the elegantly dressed crowds for a sight of him, it felt completely unreal that he would appear.

And then—he called my name.

James darted through the speeding traffic circling the Place du Carrousel. When he finally reached me, and after we'd exchanged a few shy words, he lifted me off the ground and swept me into an amazing kiss that I'd rate ten big blinking stars and another couple for sheer epicness.

I'm not the gushy type. I'm rational and logical, and not exactly prone to girly exaggeration, so when I say that kiss was like two halves of one heart meeting and locking together, you can believe me.

Or believe the cars driving past us with honking horns and people shouting out the windows, *"Vive l'amour!"*—Long live love!—and *"Eh, il ya des hôtels pour ça!"*—There are hotels for that!

My long-lost boyfriend and I stood there under the noonday sun in the center of Paris, traffic whizzing by us, ruffling our hair and sending a hot breeze up my skirt.

James's face was so open, I could see his thoughts.

"I love you," he said. I already knew.

As I said, "I love you, too," a defeated look came into his eyes.

"What's wrong?" I asked, alarmed.

James was looking over my shoulder, and I turned and saw that a black car had braked to a stop a dozen yards from where we stood. Three men leapt out. Two of them were heavily muscled and the third was tall with thick black hair that was pure white at the temples and wearing a black trench coat. He came toward us, and I saw that his face was all twisted up with fury.

He called out sharply, "James. We have to talk, son."

James turned me away from the car so that I was looking only at him. He grabbed me by my shoulders and gazed at me intensely with both love and desperation in his eyes. He said, "It's my father, Tandy. You have to run."

"No. Absolutely not. I'm not leaving you," I replied, but he begged me to do what he said.

"Please. I'll find you again. I will. But if he gets his hands on you, he'll hurt you. He'll crush you, Tandy. Just run."

Really? Run and wait another six months or a year or ten in the dark while James tries to escape his father? I think not. Maybe Mr. Rampling could hurt me, but *no one* had the power to crush me. "I have a better idea."

I fixed my eyes on the ruthless Royal Rampling and yelled, "We're not afraid of you!" I pointed an accusing finger at him and screamed, "*Ravisseur!* Kidnapper!"

James began yelling at him, too. His face was bright red, and cords stood out in his neck. "I'm not your property. I don't belong to you!"

We attracted attention, that's for sure. People streamed

toward us. Cars jammed on their brakes. Cameras and cell phones were pointed at us, and I guessed we'd hear police sirens any minute.

Mr. Rampling must've realized that, too. He scoffed, then called out to James, *"Ce n'est pas fini jusqu'à ce que je dis c'est fini."* It's not over until I say it's over.

Then he and his goons turned and stomped off to his car.

James and I stood together and watched them go.

This was a triumph, an incomparable victory.

Love had won the day.

2

Correction. Love had won the moment.

As that black car screeched away from the curb, I felt high with so many emotions: pride and elation and also fear—because while Royal Rampling had been driven away, there was nothing stopping him from coming after us again.

"Tandy," James said. "Look at me."

I looked into his gray-blue eyes, and despite the fact that his dad might still be circling around us in his car, James and I might as well have been the only two people in the world.

James smiled at me, making my heart pound.

"The look on my father's face when you stood up to him, Tandy. You are completely awesome."

We grinned at each other and hugged hard, laughing from pure delight. "We are *both* completely awesome," I said.

And we were.

Something big had changed in the last five minutes. I didn't have to fantasize. I didn't have to dream. I didn't have to sift through fractured memories looking for something real. Right now, we were in love and together—in *Paris*.

If there had been a sunset, we would have walked into it and the story would have been over. But sunset was so many hours away, and James told me he had made lots of plans.

He grabbed me into a hug, kissed my hair, and said, "You and I have some catching up to do."

I agreed. "We do."

We turned off our phones, even though my guardian, Uncle Jacob, had expressly told me never to do it. But since I was about to break at least a dozen other rules with James today—*tonight*—one more hardly made a difference.

We slipped our arms around each other, and set out on a stroll through the most romantic city in the world.

Paris was truly amazing and so incredibly different from my hometown of New York City. There were no skyscrapers. The buildings were old and grand, and a glorious river ran through the city under a clear, wide-open sky.

Could anyone ask for a better place for a reunion?

Not me. I was over the moon and the stars and even the sun.

We stopped at Depot Nicolas, a wine shop where James bought a bottle of Bordeaux wrapped in white paper. The next stop was 38 Saint Louis, where he chose a big wedge of Brie, then the Boulangerie des Deux Ponts for a long, skinny bag of warm baguettes.

We lunched on a bench under shade trees fronting the quai, a concrete embankment that slopes gently down to the River Seine. Bikers and lovers and laughing children with small dogs made an endless parade, and boats sailed by just below our feet.

We hugged and kissed, again and again, and talked over each other and laughed enough to make up for our six months of despair and total blackout. Then we went quiet.

James lifted strands of my long dark hair and wound them around his fingers. He did this reverently, as if he'd never seen my hair before. He touched the top button on my pin-tucked white shirt and traced the flouncy hem of my skirt. He kissed my temples and my mouth and the palms of my hands.

It was as if every place he touched burst into flames. I pressed my cheek to his, burrowed under his arm, and fitted myself perfectly against his strong, lean body. I ran my hand under his leather jacket and covered his fast-beating heart.

If there was ever a case of spontaneous combustion, this was it. We were on *fire*.

To tell the truth, I was so elated, I was a little afraid.

"I have something to show you," James said. "Want to take a little walk?"

He didn't have to ask me twice.

Walking hand in hand with James was like being wide-awake inside the most delicious of dreams.

He had a mischievous look on his face as he led me across the Pont des Arts, a footbridge that arched gracefully over the Seine. A low chain-link fence lined the walk, and it was festooned with padlocks—thousands of them.

James said, "Look what I have, Tandoori."

I watched eagerly as he took something out of his jacket pocket. It was an old brass padlock, as worn and dinged up as our journey to this moment. James handed the lock to me, and when I turned it over, I saw our initials etched into the back.

James did that.

I looked up at his face. His cheeks were colored with emotion, and I understood why he had brought me here. With a shaking hand, I hooked the lock into the fence between other locks that had been placed there by lovers over the years. When I closed the hasp, it made a solid and permanent sound.

James separated two keys from a ring. He gave one to me and clenched his fist around the other.

"We have to do this together," he said.

I followed his lead but turned to face him. Then he said, "On the count of three."

We smiled at each other as we counted down. At three, we heaved the little keys over each other's shoulders, beyond the sides of the bridge. They disappeared into the rushing water far below.

The moment was both joyous and solemn, as if we were taking vows that could never be broken: James Rampling and Tandy Angel together in perpetuity. Tears welled up, but I didn't want them. No more tears. I'd already shed enough tears for a sixteen-year-old girl.

James squeezed my hand, and I saw tears in his eyes, too.

It just couldn't get better than this—but it *did*.

We wandered the city for hours, just reveling in the happiness of finally being together and carefully avoiding any negative talk that could kill our buzz. When the sky turned cobalt blue, we dined alfresco on steak frites and café au lait at the Café du Trocadero. From our tiny marble table under the awnings, we had a magnificent view of the Eiffel Tower, which sparkled madly with silver lights.

Our knees touched and our feelings arced between us like lightning.

"I wrote to you," James said. "When you didn't write back, I thought you blamed me for what happened. I thought you hated me."

Of course, I hadn't known that James had written to me. At the time, I didn't even remember his name.

I told him what had happened to me since I'd last seen him: about my horrid abduction and wretched incarceration in a high-class nuthouse, the treatments that had erased him from my mind. And I told him about my parents' savage deaths. They had done everything they could to keep James and me apart, but that obstacle was gone now.

"I didn't know you had written to me until I found your cards in my mother's desk."

He covered my hands with both of his and told me about his own lockdown in a superstrict Swiss school without phones or Internet.

"My father, your parents. They did what they could to keep us apart. But this was meant to be," he said.

We left the bistro and went underground to the Métro, getting off at the St-Paul stop. We walked under warmly illuminated arches and came upon musicians playing cello and violin under the stars.

James dropped coins into the musicians' cup, and they called after us, *"Merci, monsieur et mademoiselle. Bonne chance."*

Yes, it was *phenomenal* good luck that James and I were together at last.

The next thing I knew, we stood at the entrance to a small, run-down-looking hotel called the Grand Hôtel Voltaire. The brass appointments were tarnished. The stone threshold was worn down from the millions of footsteps that had crossed it through the centuries. It was a one-star hotel, but I thought it was perfectly poetic and completely romantic.

James looked into my eyes.

And he held open the front door.

4

I was flushed and even trembling as James and I crossed the worn Persian carpets in the hotel's charming, velvet-lined lobby and stepped into a metal cage of an elevator. James slid the gate closed.

When he looked at me, I was sure he knew what I was feeling. We were in uncharted territory, James and I. Maybe he was scared, too.

All my life, my demanding parents had trained me to suppress all emotions, believing they were unnecessary distractions. But to be robbed of this intensity would have robbed me of my humanity. I was *made* to feel this way, to love James and to be loved by him.

He put an arm around me and pressed the button for

3eme étage. The creaky lift rose and stopped on the third floor with a jolt. As we walked down the hallway toward his room, James whispered, "My father can't find us now, Tandy."

We stopped at a door near the end of the hall. James pushed the key into the lock. He wiggled it. It rattled and then, finally, the door opened. I stepped into a room that was shabby but clean, smelling faintly of cigarettes.

There was a narrow bed against the wall to my right, a chair with claw feet beside it, and a tall carved armoire across from the bed that called up images of an earlier time. The one small window looked out onto Boulevard Voltaire, and enough moonlight and streetlight came through it to see by.

James hung his jacket on a hook behind the door and turned to face me. I could hardly look at him. My skin was hot, and my heart was skipping, thudding, banging against my rib cage, acting like a child on a sugar high.

I knew what James would see on my face when he looked at me: that I was *his*, only for *him*. He held my face with both hands and kissed me. It was real and tender and full of desire. He loved me. He wanted me. And I wanted him. I had never done this with anyone before, but I wasn't afraid. It felt completely right.

Fierce heat flashed through my body. He unbuttoned his shirt, and it whispered to the floor. Then he unbuttoned mine.

I'm not the kind of girl to tell others what was deeply, personally *ours*. But I can say this.

When I woke up in his bed many hours later and reached for him, I was alone.

James was gone.

I doubted my senses. Was I dreaming? I screamed out for him inside the tiny room, and then I looked in the bathroom down the hall. Back in the room, I turned on my phone and waited for it to ring. And I imagined terrible things: that James had been abducted while we slept. That he had been caged. That he was being tortured.

Then I saw the note that must have slipped from the bed and was lying on the floor. The small square of paper shook in my hand as I turned on the light. This was James's handwriting, for sure.

Dearest Tandy, he wrote, *I've been lying awake for hours watching you sleep. You are my true angel, and because I love you so much, I have to protect you. My family situation is worse than I've told you, worse than you can imagine, and I can't give my father any more reasons to hurt you or your family.*

I know this note won't be enough for you. I know you will be furious with me. But please believe this, there is no other way.

Something I read yesterday: L'amour fait les plus grandes douceurs et les plus sensibles infortunes de la vie. *Love creates the sweetest pleasures and the worst misfortunes in life.*

Don't ever doubt that I love you. And always will.
James

2

RABBIT HOLES AND BLIND ALLEYS

5

Alone, I left the Grand Hôtel Voltaire feeling as though I'd been slammed across the back of my head with a shovel, then hurled headfirst into a Dumpster.

I didn't get it. Any of it. And I was *seething.*

Why hadn't James woken me up to talk? Why didn't he trust me with what he knew and felt? Was there any truth in that note? Had he ever loved me? How could he leave me alone to figure out what had happened to us on what had been the best and worst day of my life?

Yesterday, I had thought no one could crush me.

I was wrong.

As I walked away from the hotel, I couldn't help but remember how happy I was on this same street last night with James...whoever he was, whoever I had thought he was. I hurt so much that I cried like a little kid as I navigated the streets of Paris at dawn. My family had checked out of the Hotel George V yesterday and moved into the house that had once belonged to my late grandmother, which I found with little effort.

Once "home," I went upstairs to the second-floor bathroom. I filled the bathtub and sat in the warm water for about a half hour without even moving. After that, I changed into clothes that hadn't been touched, fondled, or unbuttoned by James Rampling. I went downstairs and poured a cup of coffee, plugged in my phone to charge, and then huddled in a big leather sofa in the parlor.

Later, I heard the sounds of my family moving around the huge house, but I didn't call out. I sat on that sofa as still and as unblinking as a corpse until my little brother, Hugo, ran past with his arms outspread.

He was giving himself landing instructions—"Control tower to Hugo One, runway six is cleared for you now"—and making truly annoying engine noises. He saw me in the parlor, made a U-turn, and flung himself across my lap.

"Where were you last night?" he asked me.

"You think I have to tell *you*?"

"Jacob thought you were about to blow off the most important meeting ever. He's pretty mad."

"I was right here," I said, shoving Hugo onto the floor.

"That's a lie," he said. "Oh, I took the bedroom facing the street. Me and Matty. There's a smart TV in that room, and I can get like ninety thousand stations and post my blog."

Matty was our twenty-four-year-old big brother, Matthew Angel, cornerback for the New York Giants. Fierce, strong, as handsome as a movie star, and most of all, Hugo's hero.

At that moment, Matthew was looking out the windows into the front garden and speaking on his phone in a very animated way. In the kitchen to my right, my twin brother, Harry, was reading the back of a cracker box.

He said to me, "You're in big trouble, you know?"

Just then, our uncle Jacob stalked into the room and stood until we gave him our attention.

Shortly after our parents' sudden and gruesome deaths, just weeks before our home and all our possessions were sold to settle their debts and we were *this close* to becoming *homeless*, Jacob Perlman had appeared.

Jacob was an Israeli ex-commando and our father's long-lost oldest brother. And now he was our guardian. He was the one who had brought us to Paris to live in Gram Hilda's house and had told us about the inheritance she intended for us.

He stood in the center of this fantastic, modern-style room until our eyes were fixed on his. Then he said, "Tandy, I've told you. *Never* turn off your phone."

"Uncle Jake, believe me, I had a good reason."

"There's no exception to 'never.' We'll discuss it later."

Jacob took his wallet out of the back pocket of his khakis.

"Harry, please go out and bring back lunch for all of us. Hurry. The bankers and lawyers will be here shortly— and, kids, please trust me when I tell you to bring your A-game.

"Especially you, Tandoori. Snap out of it—whatever 'it' is. Good or bad, the results of this meeting will determine how comfortably you live the rest of your lives."

6

At half past one, nine of the seats around the mirror-polished steel table in Gram Hilda's dramatic, black-lacquered dining room were taken. We kids lined up along one side, Jacob took his seat at the head, and four gray-suited, middle-aged lawyers and bankers sat stiffly across from us.

The suits were all humorless, well pressed, and rather full of themselves. And the one who looked least likely to eat Popsicles in his underwear or sing and walk on his hands at the same time was the senior man, Monsieur François Delavergne.

Monsieur Delavergne was fat and bald, with hair shooting out of his cuffs and sprouting like weeds on his knuckles. "Pleasure to meet you," he said grimly, shaking hands with each of us.

"Don't be so sure," Hugo said.

Matty grabbed our bad boy by the shoulder. "That was rude, Hugo. Apologize."

"Just being honest," Hugo said. "Matty, are you afraid of this dude?"

Matty shook his head and said, "Sorry, Monsieur Delavergne. Hugo comes uncensored."

"Real, you mean," Hugo said. "Straight shooter, you mean."

He then bet our visitors that he could lift any of them over his head, but got no takers. Once the nonsense stopped and the presentations were under way, I turned my scattered thoughts to my beautiful, brilliant, and somewhat capricious late grandmother, Hilda Angel.

Although she died before any of us were born, we'd heard stories about her wild summer on a kibbutz when she was seventeen, her intrepid trips abroad on tramp steamers, and her high-flying life in New York and Paris.

But what we first learned about her came in the form of a scandalous handwritten codicil to her last will and testament that read, "I am leaving Malcolm and Maud $100, because I feel that is all that they deserve."

Our father had framed and hung that Big Chop—what our family not-so-affectionately calls our parents' punishments—in the stairwell near the master bedroom, where we all saw it several times a day.

Why had Gram Hilda disowned Malcolm? Maud, our very own tiger mom, had said that Hilda hadn't approved of the marriage. That must have meant Hilda hadn't approved of *her*. Maybe that was true. But I often wondered what else we hadn't been told.

I tuned back in to the men in gray as they itemized Gram Hilda's holdings, projected receipts, calculated interest rates, and translated international rates of exchange.

I followed the back-and-forth up to a point. I asked questions. I made notes, but honestly, the numbers were dense and dizzying, and although I'm a bit of a math whiz, this was a deluge of black ink and fine print with no apparent bottom line. Plus, the millions of questions and doubts about James kept slipping into my thoughts like evil weeds. I tried, but I couldn't read a single face across the table.

Were we bankrupt or not? Why were there so many papers for us to sign? Finally, I'd had enough.

"Excuse me, Monsieur Delavergne," I said. "Will you summarize, please? Uncle Jacob will explain the details to us later."

"Of course, Mademoiselle Angel," Delavergne sniffed. "Whatever you say. Whatever you want or need."

He took out a pen and a notepad from his briefcase. He said, "The grandchildren's trusts are equal. You four will each inherit"—scratching of pen on paper—"this amount."

He held up the pad so we could all see.

We four kids sucked up all the air on our side of the table. I had hoped there would be enough money in Gram Hilda's bank account to pay for our food and housing and maybe college tuition for me, Harry, and Hugo.

My most extreme wish hadn't even been close.

Delavergne went on, "But your grandmother was a careful woman. You won't get this money all at once. In fact, your inheritance will be divided into monthly payments and distributed to each of you over the next, uhh, forty-two years. Your uncle will be your executor until you each reach your majority."

"Wait," I said. "You're saying I'll get a monthly allowance until I'm fifty-eight years old?"

"Exactly," said Gram Hilda's most trusted senior attorney, *"unless you disgrace the family name."* He tapped the stack of papers the four of us had to sign.

"The degree of 'disgrace' will be determined by the five of us: Messieurs Portsmith, Simone, and Bourgogne; your uncle Jacob; and me, of course."

Really? I would be responsible to four strangers and Jacob for the next forty-two *years*?

By the way, our family was not exactly famous for following rules. So what, exactly, was their definition of *disgrace*?

"Your inheritance represents both a gift and a challenge," Delavergne continued, brightening for the first time in three hours. "That was your grandmother's guiding principle, and we expect it will become yours as well."

Once again, thoughts of James seeped into my unwilling mind. What we had was a gift and a challenge from the very beginning. And I was never one to back down from a challenge.

7

We celebrated Gram Hilda's awesome yet mysterious gifts and challenges at Alain Ducasse au Plaza Athénée, a world-class restaurant that had been awarded the maximum number of Michelin stars, and it might have rated more.

I've been to top restaurants before. I'm from *New York*. But this place was at the pinnacle of its own category.

My instant impression was that the ornate Louis XV–style dining room was like the inside of a jewelry box. The room was lined with embroidered screens. Crystals hung from wires above our heads, and there was table art on the ivory linens.

I noticed everything, but my mind was in a James

Rampling death spiral, thinking over everything we had said and done, wondering again how James could have made so many promises and then abandoned me—entirely.

Truth is, this wasn't my first collision with the unexpected and incomprehensible. My life history is shot through with bizarre events, tricks of fate, blind alleys, rabbit holes, and bonus rounds, but yesterday I had been with someone who I thought loved me unconditionally. A *partner*.

I thought my life had *changed*.

And now it had changed in a totally different way. We were financially secure, and this was such a relief, I doubt my brothers even noticed that I was underwater, drowning.

Hugo, for instance, a wildly uninhibited eater, ordered one of everything on the astonishing menu of exquisite dishes.

He confided to our waiter, "I'm very rich."

Our waiter, very smooth in a black jacket, white shirt, and bow tie, laughed and suggested to Hugo that he come to the chef's table in the kitchen, where he would be served a portion of everything he wanted.

The rest of us stayed in our seats, and over the next hour we were served outrageous delights: caviar, steamed langoustines, guinea-fowl pie, dishes flavored with "precious herbs and spices."

I merely picked at the delicacies, but I forgot about James for a few exquisite moments when I tasted the OMG *wine*. A Lafon Montrachet, it only cost about *two thousand dollars a bottle*.

"Cheers, Tandy," said my twin brother, holding up his crystal wineglass. "I really mean it. Cheers, not tears. Please let go and enjoy this spectacular night. Nothing will ever be exactly like this again."

I was wrong when I said my brothers didn't know I was suffering. Harry, sitting on my left, knew. I touched my glass to his and said, "Write me a song."

"I can only write what I'm feeling. And that's happy."

"That could work," I told Harry.

Matthew was sitting to my right. Fresh out of jail after being accused of double murder—an accusation I'd had a pretty big role in disproving—he was beaming. I made the mistake of wondering out loud what it would be like to live in Paris, and in true big-brother fashion, he doggedly staked out the opposing position.

"Tandy, you wouldn't like it here. I'd even say you'd be miserable. You'd have to wear black all the time and diet constantly, like all Parisian women do. And have you seen the young French men? Messy. Scruffy. And they smoke. All of them."

"You don't know what you're talking about, Matty," I growled. "And now you're making me mad."

Matthew laughed and held up his hands, saying, "Don't get mad, Tandy, please. Oh, listen up. I have an announcement."

As he spoke, dessert was served, and Hugo flew back to our table. Matthew clinked a silver fork against a wineglass, and when we were all staring at him over little pots of chocolate, he said, "Uncle Jacob, Tandy, little bros. My contract with the Giants has been *renewed*. So *woo-hoo*, right, guys? I'm playing football again! I'm going back to New York—"

Hugo yelled with all the air in his lungs, "Noooooooo!"

He got up on his chair and threw his arms around Matty's neck. "Don't gooooo."

"I'll call you every night," Matthew said. "I promise."

"You're going right *now*?" Harry asked. "Like *tonight*?"

"My flight takes off in three hours. I love you all. Now tell me you love me, too."

I was going to miss the hell out of my great, larger-than-life big brother. We told him so.

Wow. Something amazing just happened.

We made Matthew cry.

8

Late that night, I lay sleepless, sandwiched between goose-down blankets and silk sheets in a huge canopied bed, maybe the same bed Gram Hilda had slept in once upon a long time ago. I'd gotten past hating James Rampling and had moved halfway back to loving him again.

I couldn't help it.

I could still feel his mouth. I could still remember the way he looked at me. I was starting to think I'd been unfair.

Maybe James *hadn't* left me because he didn't love me.

He'd said he'd left me because he *did*. And there was good reason.

The last time I'd seen James, six long months ago, it had

been under circumstances both different from last night and somewhat the same.

We were alone together, but instead of lying entwined inside a small one-star hotel in Paris, we were walking in the damp sand of the Hamptons. The sea breeze was blowing through my hair, and James and I were cooling off at the edge of the ocean, not quite ready for the bed in the cottage just behind us in the dunes.

We hadn't known each other very long, but we were getting close, kissing, sharing secrets, finding out how alike we were—when headlights came out of nowhere and pinned us where we stood. And thanks to my parents and his father, that had been the last I'd seen of him, until yesterday.

So maybe what James said in his note was all true: that his father was the devil, and I wasn't safe. If I loved James, I had to trust him, right?

But would I ever see him again?

The sky was dark, and there was only the faintest moonlight coming in through the window, just as it had when James and I clutched each other in the small bed at just this time in his room last night.

I thrashed around in the enormous, luxurious bed, but there were almost too many pillows. And so I used them well, packing myself in between them so that it felt like James was holding me every way I turned.

I wound my hair around my fingers, twisted it at the nape of my neck. I opened the top buttons of my pajamas, threw the sheets and bedcovers off me. My skin was hot and tingling, and I was thinking about James.

I wondered if he was lying in bed somewhere thinking about *me*.

CONFESSION

Friend, I tried desperately to sleep as the night wore on. I couldn't find the soft spot or the quiet place in my mind, but I tried. I counted backward from a hundred. I changed positions from this way to that. I balled up the pillows. I remade the bed. I did math in my head, and I recited poetry to myself.

But I confess…no matter what I did, I couldn't stop thinking about James.

In my own defense, how could I let go of what was clearly unfinished?

I stared up at the canopy over Gram Hilda's big bed. In the dark, it glowed softly, like a blank page for writing a letter to James in my mind.

Dear James,

It's me, the very same Tandy who lay beside you last night. The note you left was, as you said, not enough for me.

You were right.

I feel lost without a map or a compass or any way to understand what has happened to us—or to find my way home.

Last night, I held nothing back. You told me you love me, and I said I love you, too. And so I just can't understand how you could leave me like this.

We aren't finished, James. Whatever your father threatens doesn't matter. Find me and tell me you won't ever leave me again.

Tandy

I imagined my unwritten, unspoken letter wafting through the window and finding its way to James.

Stranger things than that have happened.

"Good night, James," I said to myself in the dark.

I cried a little bit. Then I clutched the pillows and finally rocked myself to sleep.

9

I reached for James—and I got my arms around pillows. Only pillows.

My eyes flashed open, and with a sickening wave of disappointment, it all came flooding back: the whole twelve-hour drama of dreams fulfilled, just before they crashed, burned, dried up, and blew away, leaving me with a million questions that came down to this one: Why?

I patted the nightstand until I found my phone. It was a few minutes before six. It was just about this time yesterday morning when I'd stumbled out of the hotel as though I'd been hit with a piano and walked home alone, wondering what had really happened with James. Why had he abandoned me? Where had he gone? Would I ever see him again?

If he had left me, could I just accept that it was over?

Or was I going to torture myself with whats and whys for-freaking-ever?

I sat up in bed and looked around at Gram Hilda's room with its pale-peach-painted walls, wood-burning fireplace, and antique Aubusson carpets. I shook James out of my head long enough to think about this extraordinary many-roomed stone house, which, like Gram Hilda herself, was an intriguing mystery.

Well, I've never met a mystery I didn't want to solve.

I climbed down out of the big bed of many pillows and rooted around in my suitcase. I dressed in a pair of jeans, an NYPD T-shirt, and low-top Converse. Just in case, I grabbed my handy glow-in-the dark LED flashlight.

Jacob had told me that Gram Hilda's house had been kept just the way she had left it, the maintenance being borne by the estate. When Hugo turned twenty-one, we could direct the board to keep the house or sell it.

Meanwhile, we could use the place as we chose, except for Gram Hilda's private workroom. That was totally off-limits.

My door opened silently. I left my room, paused a moment, then stepped out into the large hallway. There was a bedroom door in the middle of each of the four walls and a narrow staircase running right through the center of the hall. Satisfied that I was the only one wandering through the house, I took the stairs up to the third floor.

The staircase ended there, emptying into a smaller hallway just under the mansard roof.

There was only one door on this floor, and when I tried the knob, it was solidly, profoundly locked. But for every lock, there's gotta be a key.

I scampered downstairs to the main foyer and found Jacob's jacket hanging in a closet. I rummaged in his pockets until I found a set of keys, then—a little bit shocked at myself, and a lot exhilarated—I darted back up to the locked door. I picked through the key ring and finally found one key that appeared to be the right size for the lock.

I was wrong, so I pawed through the keys again. My second choice fit perfectly, and when I turned the key a few times, the tumblers tripped.

I opened the door, and I've got one word for what I saw: *Whoa.*

10

As soon as the door swung open, I was hit with a powerful wave of something I can only call wonder. It was almost as if a celestial choir had burst into a drawn-out "Ahhhhhhhhhh." That's how dazed and amazed I was.

The long, airy room was white, with a beamed cathedral ceiling and tall windows on three sides. And through the window directly ahead of me, I could see a church spire behind the back garden. I smelled flowers, an amazing blend of them, and I saw silhouetted shapes of heavy furniture arrayed throughout the large room.

Gram Hilda's private workroom felt astonishing in the dark.

What had she done here? Why was it off-limits? I closed the door behind me and shot the bolt.

Once the door was locked, I patted the wall until I found the light switch. Four beautiful standing lamps flashed on, all of them topped with hat-shaped amber silk shades. Honestly, it was as though the sun had risen out of the darkness of the last heartbreaking day and night and thrown a handful of sunbeams right in front of me.

I stood with my back to the door, simply stunned by the sight of what could only be Gram Hilda's favorite things. Yeah. This room was a Hilda Angel museum.

I took a panoramic tour without moving an inch. To my left on an easel was an oil painting of a man and woman making love in a great four-poster bed. They were ecstatic. Bedding had been tossed and thrown to the floor, and their faces just radiated pleasure. I gasped a little bit, even covered my mouth. I was starting to think that maybe Gram Hilda wasn't your typical old granny.

I could hardly wait to see more.

I looked straight ahead, all the way down the length of the room to the far window. On both sides of an irregular aisle were casual groupings of upholstered chairs and exotic painted screens. To my right, lined up against the wall, were armoires, closed cabinets holding who knew what—but definitely secrets I was born to uncover.

I was suddenly struck by a powerful feeling of déjà vu, but it was as elusive as the first notes of a song you haven't heard in a long time.

I searched my mind for that ephemeral memory, and then it clicked. The scent in the air reminded me of my older sister, Katherine, who had died years ago.

And Katherine would have loved this room. Like me, she would have wanted to explore every drawer and cubbyhole.

I walked softly down the aisle of furniture so I could better see a gallery of photographs that had been hung on either side of the window.

They were breathtaking.

My gram Hilda was pictured arm in arm with a string of celebrities: Sting and Harrison Ford and Elton John. She was glamorous and beautiful, and the way these famous people looked at her, I could tell that they, too, thought Hilda Angel was a star.

There was a huge framed photo of Hilda and my grandpa Max in a formal French rose garden bounded by boxwood, and in a collection by themselves were six, no, seven photos, each of a gorgeous man wearing nothing but a smile or a satisfied look.

Gram Hilda. Were these men models? Or were they your lovers? Oh, man, oh, man. Didn't you worry you would bring disgrace upon the family name? I couldn't help laughing.

Giggling still, I tore my eyes away from the photographs, and my gaze fell on a corner cabinet that left me breathless. The cabinet was made of gleaming hardwood carved with the most adorable depictions of nude young women—nymphs, maybe—holding flowers in their arms and as parasols above their heads.

I realized that the floral fragrance was coming from this cabinet, and it freaking begged to be opened.

I flung the doors wide and ran my eyes across rows and more rows of apothecary bottles, each with a label printed with the name BELLAIRE. And beneath that, handwritten, were the names of precious oils and floral scents: myrrh, ambergris, tincture of tea rose.

I opened a deep bottom drawer and found a stack of clothbound notebooks stamped BELLAIRE in gold. Inside the books were perfume formulas and descriptions of the moods these ingredients would evoke.

I quickly deduced that Bellaire wasn't a home *parfumerie*. It was a business, with a factory in Le Marais, owned and operated by Hilda Angel.

My knees almost gave out. I clutched at a chair to

steady myself and then sat down with one of Gram Hilda's books in my hand. I saw myself napping in Katherine's bed while she did her schoolwork. She wore a fragrance called Se Souvenir de Moi, and the formula for it was written in the book I held in my lap. Se Souvenir de Moi. *Remember Me.*

Cue the celestial choir.

I'd opened a door to my grandmother's private space and not only glimpsed her secrets, I'd found memories of Katherine as well.

This was the best day of my life. This one.

11

The kitchen was in full production when, unnoticed, I returned Jacob's keys to his jacket pocket. The boys were at the table, and our uncle was dishing up omelets and pouring juice at the same time. He looked over at me as I took a seat next to Harry.

"Kids," Jacob said, "your uniforms are all in the front closet. Please change right after breakfast, because at eight on the nose, Monsieur Pierre Morel will drive you to the International Academy."

Academy? Had Jacob said *academy*?

We each shouted across the table.

Me: "Uniforms? I don't do uniforms."

Harry: "We have a driver?"

Hugo: "Why do I have to go? Didn't I tell you I'm done with school?"

Jacob turned up his iPod, slid an omelet onto his plate, poured coffee for me, Harry, and himself, then sat down to eat.

I got it. There would be no discussion.

We each found a garment bag with our name on it and whipped off the plastic covering for a look at what not to wear.

Well, the uniforms could have been worse.

I dressed in the white shirt, gray vest, gray pleated skirt, knee socks, flat shoes with a wide toe box, and a pale-gray jacket with an insignia on the breast pocket. I brushed my hair and held it back with a band. And when I returned to the parlor, Harry and Hugo were dressed pretty much like me. Trousers, of course, instead of skirts.

Monsieur Morel was about ninety years old and drove like he was a hundred and fifty. I sat in the backseat between my two brothers and watched the city slowly pass our windows until we pulled up to the school building.

"This used to be a college," Monsieur Morel informed us in heavily accented English.

But my mind was on something else. The International Academy was just across the river from the Eiffel Tower, which had been all lit up when I'd seen it last. James and

I had been bumping knees under the café table while electricity zapped our neural networks, and unfortunately it was still zapping mine.

The headmaster himself, Monsieur Avignon, met us at the door and, after a few words of greeting, hurriedly walked us to our first classes. I was obedient, even polite, but I wished like crazy that I was back in New York. That life was the way it had been before my parents died. Before I met James. When I was still a kid going to All Saints just a few blocks from the Dakota, not knowing that I was odd as hell, and that life was going to deliver some very hard knocks before I finally learned there was no place in the world where I fit in.

Like a lot of kids on their first day of school, I missed my mom. If I could have, I would have told her no one loved me.

And what would she have said? "Suck it up, Tandy. Suck it up."

12

My first-period classroom was bright and modern and had five rows of wooden tables and chairs for the students. The math teacher, Madame Mason, had the grace of a ballet dancer as she wrote out equations on a whiteboard.

I sat in the last row, looking at the gray-jacketed backs and excellent haircuts of the kids of rich and privileged foreigners stationed in Paris. My peers.

Every few minutes, one of them would turn and look at me like I was the main attraction in the weird-kid exhibit—then snap their head back to the front.

I'd been an outcast before. Welcome to my world.

I zoned out within a minute and went to a room in my mind that looked exactly like the room in the Grand Hôtel

Voltaire. I began breaking my memories of the hours I'd spent there with James into bite-sized, easy-to-digest little moments. I was thinking of James whispering, "*I love you,*" when my name seemed to boom loudly in the classroom.

I did a fast mental rewind and realized that Madame Mason had said, "Mademoiselle Angel, please explain to the class the four ways to prove that these two lines are parallel."

Twenty kids swiveled to face me.

I stood up, hoping words would jump into my mouth, but I was lost. I know geometry cold, but it was as if James had flushed all thoughts about anything but *him* right out of my head.

For an extremely long fifteen seconds, I was like an ice statue. I stared at the two lines Madame Mason had drawn on the whiteboard, and I don't think I even breathed. And then I thawed, and the four solutions to the problem came to me. I summarized the transversal postulate, explained how transverse lines intersecting parallel lines create congruent angles, and gave the answer in excellent French.

Madame Mason stared at me, dumbstruck, as though I had grown a few more heads.

I had just tucked my skirt under me and retaken my seat when there was a rush of air and movement behind me. It was Monsieur Avignon, who had burst into the classroom. I had noticed when he met us earlier that the man was jittery. Well, he was superhyper now. He pinned me with his jiggly eyes and shouted, *"Mademoiselle Angel, come with me. Immediately!"*

I stuffed my laptop into my backpack and followed the headmaster down the hall, through a set of double doors, and out to the gym, with its high echoey ceilings and hardwood floors.

I saw them immediately.

There, between workout mats and weights, were my little brother, Hugo, and another kid, who was bigger and older and was curled into a fetal position on the floor. Hugo's fists were cocked, and the boy on the floor was bloody and crying.

Hugo shouted the second he saw me.

"This punk said we killed Malcolm and Maud. I told him to take it back. Or else. He wouldn't do it, Tandy."

The weird, maybe scared looks from my classmates made some kind of sense now. They thought we were *killers.* A nurse and a doctor ran toward the moaning kid on the floor, and then Harry drifted in and, in no particular hurry, came over to me.

"Whassup," said my twin brother.

His pupils were huge, and he had a dopey expression on his face. What the hell?

I whispered, "Harry. Are you *stoned*?"

"Sit over there," said Monsieur Avignon, pointing to some folding chairs. "Monsieur Perlman is coming now."

Oh, crap. We were *really* in for it now.

13

Jacob stood in the center of the parlor and looked at us with the hard eyes of a commando. When his expression was cold, it meant that under the surface, he was ripping mad, and oh, man, I do not like it when Jacob is mad.

The three of us had sunk down in square leather chairs, Harry and I guilty by association with Hugo because we'd taken a stand. If Hugo had to leave the International Academy, we'd all go with him.

And Hugo was defiant.

"You can't expect me to let people accuse us of murdering Malcolm and Maud," our little brother said. "Uncle Jake, would *you* take that?"

"I don't expect you to throw the first punch, Hugo. I

don't expect you to bait other people into throwing the first punch, either."

"When you've been insulted, the first punch is a technicality," said Hugo. "And I'm not apologizing to that shit, even if his father *is* the king of France."

"Hugo. All of you. You just don't get it. Your inheritance is *conditional* on good behavior. Monsieur Delavergne used his contacts to get you into that school, and now, Hugo, you thanked him by pooping in the punch bowl."

Hugo cracked up. He started repeating, "I pooped in the punch bowl," until he was rolling on the floor with tears in his eyes. Before Jacob seized him by the belt and the back of his neck, I jumped to my feet.

"Define 'disgrace,' Jacob, because I don't get that. Or is it in the fine print of page one thousand forty-three of that document I signed?"

"Sit down, Tandy."

"I prefer to stand."

"Sit. *Down*."

I sighed. I threw myself back down into the chair and looked up at him like, "What?"

"You want me to define 'disgrace'? If that boy's parents go to the media or hire a lawyer, you can bet that's a disgrace. I have one vote, kids. One vote. If you don't get yourselves under control, you're not going to like the repercussions."

Harry said, "Maybe we could make the problem disappear, Jacob. If Hugo apologizes, could you ask Monsieur Avignon to give us another chance? If he takes us back, no problem, right? I liked the school."

"Of course you did. You bought marijuana outside the front door, and, Harry, that's not only a disgrace, it's a crime."

"Oh. Monsieur Morel told you. You're spying on us?" Harry said. "I'd call *that* disgraceful, Jake."

"Go to your rooms," our uncle said. "Leave your phones on the kitchen table. I'm disconnecting the Wi-Fi."

Hugo shouted, "Nooooooooo!"

Jacob gave me a look that made me feel like a bug. A small bug. About to be squashed. He said, "And by the way, Tandy, don't go into my pockets again."

Jacob went on, "You're all grounded. Think of this house as lockup until I find a school that will take you."

The three of us left the parlor. In disgrace.

I had no plans to leave the house. After this, I wouldn't dare, but as I slunk off to my room, I had no idea that before morning, I would be taking a trip into the *past*. And in the process, I would get one of the greatest shocks of my life.

3

A GHOST STORY

14

I have to prepare you for something I wasn't prepared for myself.

I never expected to run into the ghost of my dead sister.

The night we were kicked out of school was a waking nightmare. I couldn't sleep for thinking about Gram Hilda's stiff-necked lawyers and bankers, who looked unforgiving and vengeful.

I thought about Hugo's incorrigible fighting, and then Harry buying dope right outside school. It wasn't exactly the action of a casual smoker. And the worst for me, personally, was Jacob's disappointment in me for filching that key.

The three of us had been awful. Jacob didn't deserve that, and we all knew it.

I stared at the canopy for hours. I was sweaty and pissed off at myself and beyond restless, and at just after midnight, when I couldn't lie in bed for another minute, I got up, put on my Converse, and grabbed a flashlight.

I wasn't going to borrow any keys, but I was determined to map out my grandmother's house from the basement to her attic atelier. This was partly my house. So what could possibly be wrong with taking a stroll?

I crept past Jacob's room, then tiptoed down the center stairs, and when I got to the kitchen, I took a sharp right. I'd seen a door at the end of the pantry and was pretty sure it opened onto a staircase that led down to the cellar.

And yes, indeed, it did.

The pantry door opened easily, and cool air rushed toward me as I went down the stairs. When I got to the bottom, I swung my flashlight around until I found a chain attached to a light fixture in the ceiling.

I pulled the chain, and the light came on, revealing a stone basement room with a furnace in the corner. To my left was an old door with strap hinges and an old latch. My detective instincts told me there would be something interesting behind it.

The latch was locked, but I pried it open with a rusty

bar, only breaking two fingernails in the process. But I didn't care at all. The room within a room was a mystery enclosed in an enigma.

I was standing inside a stone chamber that had once been a wine cellar, but there was no wine. There was something much better.

Right in front of me was a monastery table made of heavy, hand-cut planks, and on the table, centered and squared, were three cardboard bankers' document boxes.

I had to know what was inside those boxes. Why had they been stored in an airless basement room? Would I find more racy photographs inside? Or were they filled with old journals, secret tales by Gram Hilda?

I walked to the table and put my hand on the box closest to me and turned it so that light fell on the label.

A name had been written in marking pen.

KATHERINE

That was my sister's name. My sister who had *died*.

15

I *was seriously freaked out at* reading my sister's name. I turned the other two boxes around and, yeah, each one was marked KATHERINE.

They had to belong to some *other* Katherine.

My sister had died in a horrific motorcycle crash in South Africa six years ago. Nothing belonging to her could possibly have found its way to my grandmother's basement. Right?

Whether that was right, wrong, or something else, I had to find out what was inside these boxes.

The lids were sealed with transparent packing tape. I grabbed the first box and pulled at the tape with my broken nails—then I lifted the lid.

Right inside the opened box was a large white envelope. There was no writing on it and the flap wasn't sealed. I worked my fingers into the envelope and pulled out a contact sheet, a page of thumbnail-sized photographs.

My heart started banging again.

It was Katherine. My Katherine.

The overhead lightbulb was perfect for scrutinizing small items, and I closely examined the twenty-four tiny pictures of my beloved sister. She was alone in each snapshot, and in every one of them, she looked as beautiful and as happy as the last time I saw her.

And *snapshot* is the right word, as in *candid snapshot*. None of the pictures were posed. Katherine didn't seem aware that she was being photographed, so the photographer had to have been hidden. Or else the photographer had captured her on film with a zoom lens, paparazzi-style.

And that wasn't all.

These pictures had been taken in Paris. Not New York, not Cape Town. *Paris*.

Had Katherine stopped off here before she'd had the fatal collision with a tractor-trailer in Cape Town? Had she left these boxes, planning to send them home to New York? The stone walls of the subterranean basement room were starting to close in on me. I was in a tomb with the last pictures of Katherine, but I couldn't leave. Not yet.

I put the pictures down and plunged my hands into the box.

There were more envelopes and accordion folders, the kind that hold thick packets of paper. I opened everything hurriedly.

I saw stacks of papers that had Katherine's name on the cover sheets, but before I could read them, I saw a *chart* with her name printed across the top. I'd seen charts like these before. They had been in my father's home office, labeled with the names of each of my siblings, and of course, there was a chart with my name, too.

This chart of Katherine's was dated only weeks before her death.

There were codes down the left-hand side, numbers across the bottom, dates across the top. I could read these charts in my sleep. I did it now, and I was as far from sleep as I had ever been in my life.

In a period of one year, Katherine's IQ had shot up from 133 to more than 180. It was off the charts.

As for her physical capacity, Katherine had run a mile in four minutes. Was that a record for a sixteen-year-old girl? It could well be. The next column showed that at her last testing, Katherine had bench-pressed four hundred forty pounds. That was out of the ballpark and over the top.

I stared at the colored lines on the graph and noted the

steep incline of the upward trend. And I had a good idea what had caused all this "progress."

A shadow fell across me, and reflexively, I put the chart behind my back as I spun around.

Jacob said patiently, "We'll talk about Katherine, you and I. But not tonight, Tandy. You're going to a new school in the morning, and you're *not* going to be late."

16

Monsieur Morel, Jacob's spy and our ancient chauffeur, stopped the car in front of our second school in two days. It was behind a high stone wall that had a statue of the Virgin Mary atop the pediment. I saw the shape of the building behind the gates. It had a dome with a crucifix on top—and I understood what Jacob had done.

He had enrolled us in a convent school. We would be going to a school run by nuns.

School was the last place I wanted to be. Do you know the feeling? And a religious school? That hadn't even been a blip on my radar.

I guess our uncle was offsetting our expulsion from the

International Academy, maybe trying to score points with Gram Hilda's board of lawyers and bankers. Or maybe this was the only school in Paris, France, that would take the three Angel kids, who'd been accused of killing their parents.

Either way, the lesson for the day was "Don't mess with Jacob."

Monsieur Morel opened the rear passenger door for me while Hugo kicked the other one open and spilled out onto the street with Harry. Our Yoda-like driver smiled and said, "I'll be here at three, Mademoiselle Tandy."

I said, "Okay," but I was wasting none of my charm on Morel. I wanted to get back to the boxes of my sister's stuff in the basement, but I couldn't buck Uncle Jacob. Not today.

The three of us were buzzed through the gates and then entered the convent school of the Sisters of Charity. It was a bare-stone building inside and out. A nun, who didn't introduce herself, took us to the office of the school administrator, Sister Marie Claire.

Sister Marie Claire was nothing like the glossy fashion mag she shared her name with. She was about fifty, maybe older, wearing the full nun habit from starched cap to sturdy black shoes. She gave us papers to fill out, then spent an hour explaining the rules of the school. No jewelry, no shouting, no cursing, no phones—it went on and on.

"Your first class every day will be advanced French, and I will meet with you every afternoon at last period for theology. I am to report any...how do you say?" She searched her memory, and we waited to hear what she had to report.

"I am to report any 'shenanigans' to Monsieur Perlman," Sister Marie Claire said. "But I am also here as your adviser. You may always come to me."

Hugo said, "Yeah, right."

The sister walked behind him and slapped the back of his head, hard.

"Yow! That hurt!" Hugo bellowed.

I stood up and grabbed Hugo in a protective hug. Sister Marie Claire clutched my biceps with a talon grip and told me, "Take your seat, Mademoiselle Angel. Immediately."

I did what she said, shooting glances at Harry and Hugo as I did so. The three of us were flustered and frightened. The sister had only reinforced the fears I'd had from the moment I saw the forbidding walls around this convent.

Our real life in Paris had just begun.

Hugo, Harry, and I went to class. We paid attention, and speaking for myself, I did my best to make Jacob proud.

68

Actually, I thought my brothers also got the message, but in the afternoon, when I was aching for a dismissal bell to ring, Sister Marie Claire tapped me on the shoulder and told me to go to the chapel.

"Father Jean-Jacques is waiting to hear your confession," said the nun.

CONFESSION

Picture a chapel not much bigger than the parlor in Gram Hilda's house. An agonized Jesus Christ was nailed to a huge crucifix behind the altar. The gray stone walls and floor chilled the air inside.

And there was a confessional off to one side. It even had a shaft of prismatic light hitting it from above. Oh, man, I didn't like the looks of it at all. I was baptized, but our family had never been the kind who went to church or confessed our sins. I'm pretty sure Malcolm and Maud refused to believe they had any to confess.

I slouched over to the confessional and opened the door, took a seat, and crossed myself. I knew I was supposed to have examined my heart and my sins and experienced genuine remorse, but my conscience, such as it is, had never been cleaner.

I spoke in French, saying, "Bless me, Father, for I have sinned," because I knew I was supposed to say that, and then I added, "It's been about a hundred years since my last confession."

A deep voice with a bit of a laugh in it said, "I've got all day to hear your century of sins. I am also available tomorrow."

Nuts.

Now I was committed to blowing Father Jean-Jacques's cassock off, and I was *not* going to censor myself. I closed my eyes, held my nose, and jumped off the board into the deep end.

"Well, Father, in the last century, I have spied on people and defied people. I have been rude to the police and have shown them up and proven them wrong. I have bragged about being smart, and separately, I have brought disgrace on the family name. That's what I've been told. And even though my parents and his disapproved, I had a boyfriend. *Had*. Past tense. But he was my boyfriend, all right. Use your imagination, Father, because I don't kiss and tell. But I loved him and he loved me and we were together, with all that that implies."

There was silence from the other side of the screen, so I continued. Actually, I was missing James again like crazy, and I wasn't ready to stop talking about him.

"I earned having a boyfriend, Father, because this boy was my first love, and I had a pretty crappy upbringing disguised as intellectual enrichment. My siblings and I were used as guinea pigs. That's right. Guinea pigs—as in lab animals.

"Our parents fed us drugs that were off-the-charts weird, and they made us different from any other kids in the world. You can believe me or not. Make of that what you will. But I'm an original, Father. And if God made me, I was tinkered and tampered with by my parents, who also made me. All of us Angels were messed with, Father. I think we were subjected to sins against nature. For years."

I took a breath and croaked out, "If there's a God, he knows I'm doing the best I can."

I was winded and a little bit weepy because I'd never told this story in this way to anyone before. It was plenty of stuff, maybe enough to give Father Jean-Jacques a heart attack.

But I didn't hear a heavy *thunk* on the stone floor.

The man behind the screen said, "Is that all, child? Is that supposed to be—a dare? Are you daring God to love you?"

I pondered that for a long time. "Yes, I suppose so, Father." My voice was so small.

The priest said, "He loves you. Don't worry about that."

I told the priest I had nothing to be contrite about and added, "I don't do penance and I never will."

I could almost hear the priest thinking what to do with me, maybe throw me out and kick my butt for good measure.

After a long pause, Father Jean-Jacques said, "While God loves you and forgives you, you must still acknowledge the sin in your heart, and I believe you are doing this, child. I heard how you listed those sins. So I have an idea.

"For now, rather than penance, please meditate for fifteen minutes a day on things you have done to hurt other people, and I think this may help you heal from your parents' betrayal against nature. And against *you*."

I was quiet. Choked up, actually, but I didn't want Father to know.

"Everyone at the Sisters of Charity is praying for you. God bless you," he said.

About five minutes later, I got into our hired car, and my brothers followed at fifteen-minute intervals, each of them looking quite sober. As if we'd been thrown into cold showers and then rubbed down hard from head to toe with warm towels.

I don't know what that looks like, actually.

But call me surprised. I felt pretty okay.

17

After blowing up our enrollment at the International Academy, we knew enough to follow the overly strict and somewhat arbitrary rules at the convent school.

Our first school week was short, but *sooooo* boring, it seemed like it went on forever. We knew the course work, yeah, even Hugo knew his. Our parents, with all their faults, hadn't raised stupid children.

One good thing is that I've been following the priest's orders to meditate on how I've hurt people. It's helped me recognize that we can't help but make mistakes, even when our intentions are good. Of course, my parents took that way too far, but maybe I'll be able to completely forgive them one day. I never thought I'd say that, so that's progress.

And that is absolutely all I can say for the start of my junior year under the heavy thumbs of the Sisters of Charity.

That Friday afternoon, after making sure Jacob wasn't home, I took Harry down to the basement. I jerked the chain on the light fixture that lit up the empty cellar, and Harry pulled out a joint from his back pocket. Before I could stop him, he lit up.

"Are you *crazy*?" I shrieked at him.

"Well, yeahhhhhh. It runs in the family," he said mildly. "I thought you knew that."

"Put it out. It's going to stink down here. Jacob is going to know, and he's going to make us very sorry."

Harry inhaled deeply, then pinched out the end of the joint and put it back in his pocket. I glared at him as he finally exhaled, but he wasn't contrite.

Recently, I'd sensed that Harry was becoming bolder, more sure of himself. He was writing a lot, definitely composing music, and given his extraordinary talent, he was probably creating something quite special. When I asked him what he was working on, all he said was "Stuff is cooking, sis. But it's not done yet."

"Weed is bad for you," I went on, stating what I was pretty sure was obvious. "I can cite you a hundred articles on the deleterious effects of marijuana on the adolescent brain."

He looked at me and then cracked up.

That idiot said, "I think the damage was done before I smoked *this*."

He checked out the room. Then he walked up to the closed door on the left, the one with the old strap hinges. And as I had done earlier, he pried open the latch.

"Whatever you want me to see is in here, right?" he said.

I pushed him aside, pulled open the door, and grabbed the lightbulb chain.

Harry went directly to the hand-hewn table and the three cartons with Katherine's name written in bold black marking pen. He sucked in air and said, "Whoa, Tandy. Katherine? Not *our* Katherine? I'm not sure about this."

With my twin right beside me, I opened the first box and pulled out our sister's chart.

"Take a look," I said.

His eyes got huge and focused. I could see that his dope high was largely gone. He stared at the chart, took it out of my hands, and read the symbols and dates on both the X and the Y axis of the graph. Then he looked at me, completely sobered—and there was no question about what we both knew.

Katherine had been on the pills, some of the same ones I had been on, some of the same ones that had been fed to

Harry and to Hugo. And she'd been dosed with the pills for speed and agility that Matthew had gobbled down all his life.

Harry's voice cracked right down the middle when he said to me, "We should have guessed. They did it to her, too."

I put my finger on the trend lines and traced their jagged upward climb. "Look at this, Harry. She was smarter than Stephen freaking *Hawking*. She was stronger than Matty and Hugo."

"Did you have any idea?" he asked me.

I shook my head no.

"What's in the other boxes?"

"Raise your hand if you want to find out," I said.

18

I handed Harry the sheet of thumbnail-sized photos of Katherine walking around Paris, seemingly oblivious to the photographer. Harry held them under the bare bulb and burst into tears.

He was crying as he said, "I don't understand this at all. She wasn't supposed to be in Paris. Who took these pictures?"

I mumbled, "I don't know, I don't know," and after my brother wiped away his tears with the backs of his hands, we looked over the reports with our sister's name on the covers. Behind the cover sheets, we found letterhead from Angel Pharmaceuticals, the company our father owned with our wretched uncle Peter.

"Bet you a million euros they told Kath she was taking *vitamins*, like they did with us," Harry said.

I was opening more envelopes when I found another contact sheet of pictures. Harry grabbed it and held it under the bare bulb. I yelled, "Hey!" then stared at it from behind his shoulder. Katherine's hair was the same length as in the other photos, but she was wearing a different shirt, jacket, and scarf.

And there was a boy in some of the pictures.

He had his arms around Katherine. He looked at her adoringly. I felt my stomach clench—had James looked at me that way? I blocked that thought.

We knew Katherine had been with a boy named Dominick when she'd been killed in South Africa. But these pictures were taken in Paris.

"That's got to be Dominick," Harry said. "Couldn't be anyone else. Sis, did Kath stop off in Paris before going to Cape Town? Did she meet Dominick here?"

"My questions exactly," I said.

My eyes burned with tears as I saw my teenage sister with the dark-haired boy. They looked euphoric. Harry had to be right. Dominick had to be the boy Kath had written about while she was on her Grande Gongo—aka a major reward my parents gave for overachieving—in Cape Town. She'd said she loved him.

"Check my memory of this," I said. "Dominick was never seen after the accident. But it was assumed that he survived the crash, right? I remember Dad going over there, turning the city upside down looking for him."

"What I mostly remember is how hard you took the news, even with your zero-emotion pills," said Harry.

I nodded, my throat dry. I don't think I'll ever truly get over losing her.

Harry began emptying the third cardboard box. He was flushed and wheezing through his asthma-challenged lungs.

The thing about twins, even ones like us who aren't telepathic, is that without reading the other's actual thoughts, we each knew what the other was thinking.

Harry and I both realized we had to get to the bottom of this mysterious cache of documents before Jacob caught us with our hands in the cookie jar.

19

The brown, letter-sized envelope at the bottom of the third and last box looked dirty. It was rumpled and maybe sticky, as if it had been carried around for a while, possibly rolled up and used to swat flies.

Harry and I went for it at the same time, but I got it first.

I held it out so he could see that there was no address on the front; then I turned it over. A name and address were written faintly in pencil on the back. It was as though the writing was an afterthought.

I read out loud, " 'D. Tremaine,' " and added, "and there's a street address in Montmartre."

There was no cell phone coverage in the cellar, so checking out this lead would have to wait. Meanwhile, I saw that the envelope's flap had been sealed and opened repeatedly, and while it looked unsavory, it was at the same time irresistible.

Harry hung his head over my shoulder, mouth-breathing as I pulled out the scant contents of the envelope.

The first paper was a bill, an invoice from a detective agency in New York called Private, addressed to Peter Angel at his home address, also in New York. The charges were not itemized, just a flat fee of nine thousand dollars "for services rendered"; the invoice had been stamped PAID.

A private detective had been hired to do what? Why? And why was this invoice in a box of Katherine Angel artifacts secreted in Gram Hilda's basement?

Had Peter hired this private eye when my father was unsuccessful in his hunt for Katherine's boyfriend?

I put the invoice down on the table and went back to the brown envelope. I stuck my hand in again and pulled out three individual sheets of paper that were clean and bright. I ran my eyes over them fast, but still, I caught the salient point.

"I don't believe this," I said to Harry.

"Show me," he said, making a grab for the papers, which I yanked out of his reach.

"Just show me!" he shouted.

I did. Each of the three sheets was embossed with letterhead in Hebrew letters. But the typed portions were in English: three individual authorizations for payment to Private for three thousand dollars each. The signature read *Jacob Perlman*.

I said, "What the hell? Was the Israeli army interested in Katherine? If so, why? And if not the army, what was Jacob's interest in Katherine?"

Harry said, "We met Jacob for the first time three months ago when Uncle Peter sent him to take over the rotten job of babysitting us. It always struck me as suspicious that a man like Jacob would take that job."

"I don't know why Jacob was kept as a big dark secret," I said slowly. "Why didn't Malcolm ever tell us he had an older brother?"

"We have to think of Jacob with a big question mark over his head from now on," said Harry.

I suddenly felt faint and nauseous. I stood so that my back was against the wall, the flats of my hands pressing the cold, rough stone. I saw flickering lights that weren't really there and felt like an ice pick was pushing through my brain toward the back of my right eye.

I'd only had a migraine once before, and I quickly realized I'd been exposed to a bunch of triggers that could set one off: extreme stress, lack of sleep, change of diet, even change of environment, like the dry air in this basement room.

My vision was narrowing. Harry's voice was way too loud, and yet I knew he was talking very softly. Was there time to stop this head-bomb with a pill?

I moved toward the monastery table like I was walking underwater. I slid the paid bill from Private along with Jacob Perlman's authorizations back into the dirty brown envelope. I grabbed the contact sheet picturing Kath and the boy who might have been her lover, and slid that into the envelope, too.

Then I tucked the envelope into the waistband of my skirt and hid it under my blouse.

Meanwhile, Harry was stacking unread reports back inside the boxes. The sound of him pulling tape off the roll was like the roar of a tornado coming at me down a highway.

"You okay?" Harry asked.

"No."

Harry taped the boxes closed, and when the room

looked tidy enough to pass military inspection, he took my hands. "I'm right here, Tandy. Let's go."

He turned off the lights and locked up behind us, and we got the hell out of Dodge before the migraine could knock me to the floor.

20

I was in Gram Hilda's bed with the lights out when Jacob came into the room again to check on me.

"Feeling better?" he whispered.

I told him my migraine was about the same size but with less intensity behind my eyes.

"Try to sleep. I'll bring you another ibuprofen in an hour."

He very gently adjusted the goose-down blankets and curtains, squeezed my hand, and then quietly closed the door.

I did some relaxation exercises, especially the one where you imagine yourself in a place where you were once happy.

I remembered being happy whenever I jumped into Kath's bed at night after dinner. I'd snuggle up to her while she read histories of Western civilization and philosophy, and she would sometimes say, "Listen to *this*, Tandy."

She had told me secrets about boys and her dreams of a life beyond school. And I remembered the way she smelled: Se Souvenir de Moi.

But just before dozing off to pleasant memories, I jumped awake with memories of my mother's screams the day we found out Katherine was dead. Images followed: Malcolm and Maud, their faces gray as they told their four remaining children what little they knew about our sister's death. I remembered Matty smashing chairs and glassware as Hugo howled.

I remembered sitting on the floor with my shocked and terrified twin outside the master bedroom door, seeing Maud in bed with a migraine, and Malcolm silently stuffing clothing into a duffel bag, rushing past us with a phone to his face, calling our driver to come around with the Bentley.

The next thing I remembered was Katherine's funeral. The coffin was closed, of course. I didn't like to think about that. I spoke at my sister's graveside, or maybe it would be more accurate to say I stood at my sister's graveside and, although I had things I wanted to say, I just sobbed. I didn't remember what anyone said, exactly, but there were dozens of heartfelt good-byes.

But now, in the present, I was awake, and I wanted to know everything about my sister from my current perspective.

Before I opened the cardboard boxes, I'd never thought the story of Katherine's death was the slightest bit questionable.

Now questions had been raised.

I thought about Katherine in Paris and the boy named Dominick who had never been found dead or alive in Cape Town. I thought of my uncle Peter, the head of Angel Pharmaceuticals. And I pictured Katherine taking the many, many pills that the adults in our family had conspired to give her—for reasons of their own.

Malcolm and Maud held many principles—but honesty wasn't one of them. They had lied to us about the drugs. They had lied about Maud's business so that it was an utter surprise of the *holy crap* kind when we found out that her company was under siege, and the same could be said for Angel Pharmaceuticals.

Now I felt certain we hadn't been told the whole truth of Katherine's death. Maybe everything we knew about that was a lie.

21

The next morning, my head was clear and pain free, but my hands still shook and my legs wobbled. I clutched the banister and hobbled down a flight of stairs to Harry's room. He'd obviously been working all night. I pushed sheet music off his bed and tickled him awake.

"You said you wanted in on this," I told him, waving the dirty brown envelope in his face.

"What's the plan?"

It took about a minute and ten seconds to reach the number listed as belonging to D. Tremaine. Harry's ear and mine were both pressed hard to a side of my phone when the call was answered.

I asked, *"Est-ce Dominick Tremaine?"*

"*C'est Dominick. Qui est à l'appareil?*"

Afterward, Harry and I dressed quickly and neatly. I even put on some lipstick. Jacob was very kind at breakfast. He looked into my face, really studied it. I smiled.

"I'm okay," I said. "I feel really good."

He said, "Good recovery, Tandy." He smiled and sprinkled crushed nuts on my oatmeal. Poured me a big mug of milky coffee.

"We're going to the Louvre," I said. "If it's okay."

Harry added, "We're going to rent headsets and do the masters the right way."

Jacob gave us each some folding money and said, "Your phones are charged, right? Make sure. Call if you need me. Have fun and please be home in time for dinner."

When we were on the street, Harry and I caught a cab at the queue and sped off to Montmartre. It was an artsy village on a very famous hill that was rife with cafés, street musicians, and landmarks, especially la Basilique du Sacré Coeur, a church with an unparalleled view of Paris out to the horizon.

But Harry and I had no time for sightseeing or leisurely strolls through the postcard vignettes of Paris. We were on a quest, wherever it took us, and with luck, we'd still have time to see the Mona Lisa before dinner.

Dominick Tremaine's address was on one of the seamier streets in Montmartre; it was narrow, twisting, and, according to my street app, notorious for sex shops and prostitution. Our cabdriver looked at us well-dressed, clean-faced twins in his rearview mirror and asked, *"Dois-je attendre?"*

"Thanks, but don't wait. We'll be okay," I said in French, hoping it was the truth.

Harry pushed euros into the driver's hand, and we hopped out of the cab at the foot of a winding street banked by shuttered residential buildings with crummy shops and bistros on the ground floors. I saw a painted sign with a street name and led the way up steps cut into the side of the street until we reached a doorway that listed names of tenants beside corresponding apartment numbers and buttons.

We rang, and the door buzzed open. Harry took the lead as we climbed two steep staircases. I was panting when we reached the top landing, maybe because I suddenly realized what we had done. Harry and I were alone in a strange place. No one knew where we were, and we were knocking on the door of the man who had probably been the last person to see Katherine alive.

Had he been her lover?

Had he gotten her killed?

How would he react to seeing Katherine's younger sibs?

Harry rapped on the door. I heard the sound of shoes on a hardwood floor, and then the door opened a crack. A dark eye looked at us for long seconds; then the door closed, hard.

"*Wait,*" I said.

But I'd jumped the gun. A chain slid along a track, and this time when the door opened, there was a very good-looking man in his mid- to late-twenties standing in the doorway.

In fact, he looked the way my brother Matthew had warned me French men all looked.

Dominick's black hair was uncombed and falling loose to his shoulders. He hadn't shaved in a couple of days, and it looked as though he'd slept in his clothes.

But although he looked older, rougher, and, I have to say, sadder, I recognized this man from the photos I'd seen of him with Katherine. I said in French, "We spoke on the phone this morning. I'm Tandy Angel, and this is my brother Harry."

He said, "You are alone?"

"Yes."

He said, "You speak French almost as well as Katherine. *S'il vous plaît, entrez.*"

22

Dominick's flat was as comfy as an old sweater.

The sitting room had three dormer windows, each with a sliver view of Sacré Coeur. The walls were lined with bookshelves, filled with probably five or six thousand books with tattered jackets, either secondhand or just really well read, on subjects ranging from fine art and architecture to history, astrophysics, astronomy, and even poetry.

An orange cat sprawled on a two-seat sofa opposite a lounge chair. Books and manuscript boxes were piled on the floor alongside the chair, and there was another short stack on a side table, along with a laptop and a gang of pill bottles.

Dominick shooed the cat away, offered us the love seat, then brought over an opened bottle of wine and three glasses.

I was pretty sure wine would reignite my headache big-time, but I held the glass in my lap, and in a few sentences, I gave Dominick the shortest credible explanation for why we were in Paris. I explained that our parents had died, that our deceased grandmother had owned a home in the Sixteenth Arrondissement, and that our guardian had brought us to Paris to help settle family affairs.

"Not your uncle Peter?" Dominick asked.

"No. Our uncle Jacob. Kath told you about Peter?"

Dominick dipped his head, and his hair fell across his eyes. I couldn't read him, and by then Harry was saying, "We found your name and pictures of you with our sister in our grandmother's house."

Dominick nodded and said, "I'm glad you found me. I've had no one to talk to about Katherine. This has been killing me for so long."

He got up, took a framed photo off the wall, and brought it over to the love seat. Tears jumped into my eyes. I couldn't help it. The photo was a *gasper*.

Dominick was astride a big honkin' motorbike, like a souped-up Harley. His hair was pulled back in a pony, he wore tight black leathers, and his face radiated joie de vivre. Our dear Katherine was on the seat behind him, her arms tightly wound around his waist, a helmet capping her long hair. She looked so happy, and you could just see that she loved and trusted this man.

This photo could have been a poster for a romantic comedy slash road-trip movie with a happy Hollywood ending.

Dominick said, "We were in Cape Town. I handed my phone to a stranger on the street and he snapped this. This is the last picture of my dearest love. Your sister, Katherine."

23

I held the picture with both hands and stared into my sister's face. I saw no fear, no premonition that she was about to die. All I could see was that she was in love. That she was having the adventure of her life.

The orange tabby settled onto Dominick's lap as I asked him to please tell us what had happened the day Katherine died.

Dominick stroked the cat and gave a long sigh.

He said, "I had met Katherine through friends in New York, and when she won the Grande Gongo, she called me. We arranged for her to stop over in Paris, then travel to South Africa together."

Dominick reminisced about the trip from Paris, the long

journey to the alluvial mines outside Karasburg. His face actually relaxed as he told us about the day Kath found a large and enviable diamond "ten carats in the rough."

"We were on the bike, going from a jeweler in Malmesbury back to Cape Town. We were traveling on a highway, at a safe speed, when without warning—no horn, no sound of brakes—we were slammed from behind. I never saw the bus that hit us," Dominick said.

He looked dazed as he told us, as if he was repeating a story he'd seen from a distance rather than experienced.

"Much later I was told that we were sent flying over the divider into the oncoming traffic and that a bus rammed into the bike. *Mon dieu*. I'm sorry to even tell you this now."

This much of the story I already knew. But what had happened after the collision?

"I must have been thrown free when the bus hit us. I only know that I was in the hospital for a long time."

He pulled up his pants legs and showed us brutal scars up to his knees. He shook his head violently, remembering.

"I had a concussion, broken bones, internal bleeding, and when I finally woke up, I learned that Katherine had been thrown into a fuel truck, which then exploded. And that she was dead.

"I was given a note from someone who had attempted

to see me in the hospital. You know this man," Dominick said.

"Our father?" Harry asked. We both knew that Malcolm had gone to Cape Town looking for Katherine's boyfriend.

"Not your father. His brother. It was Peter Angel," said Dominick. "The note was short and cutting, cursing me, saying the accident was my fault. At first I thought he must be suffering the loss of Katherine as much as I was."

Dominick was weeping now. He tried to speak, but his sobs overwhelmed him. At last, he said, "To accuse *me...* I was hit from behind. From *behind*. The bike flew like a rocket into the truck. *Flew*. That's what I was told."

Tears were rolling down my cheeks, and there was nothing I could do to stop them. Dominick's story was like an incredibly vivid dream, the worst kind of nightmare. But after we both wiped tears away, I asked him to tell me more about the note.

"Peter Angel wrote that I was never to approach your family for any reason. To keep to myself. To never speak of the accident or of Katherine—or I would pay with my life. He said he had the means to have me *killed*.

"I was a broken man. I thought of suicide many times, but I knew Katherine wouldn't have wanted me to do that. My mother would have been destroyed. I have a sister also, and she was about to be married. I couldn't bear to hurt her.

"I came back to Paris," Dominick told us. "I stay here at home where I can see the church and hear the bells. And I can remember that Katherine sat where you are sitting. That she found and named this cat when he was a kitten. Red Boy. I remember how we listened to music and laughed.

"I have never stopped loving Katherine," Dominick said, his voice dissolving again into awkward sobs.

Harry and I were also breaking down, using our sleeves to mop up the tears.

CONFESSION

Like a trigger, when Dominick tearfully said he had never stopped loving Katherine, my mind suddenly filled with images of James.

I couldn't help imagining that James was here in this room now, sitting beside me. This James, the one in my daydream, saw how the loss of love had devastated Dominick. And seeing that, he promised himself—and me—that he would never let me out of his sight.

I saw him in my mind, turning to me, fixing me with his gray-blue eyes, then pulling me to my feet and wrapping me in his arms, holding me so tightly it almost hurt.

And, friend, I could almost hear him say the words I needed to hear and believe.

"I won't ever let you go again, Tandy. Whatever happens, we'll face it together."

I imagined my reply.

"I'm yours, James. Always."

Would James come back to me?

Was there more to our story?

There had to be. There just had to be more.

24

Harry and I arrived back home before dinner and told Jacob about the awesome Givenchy and Monet exhibitions at the Louvre, which we'd seen at a really fast run just before the museum closed for the day.

Naturally, we omitted telling our uncle about interviewing Katherine's earnest and heartbroken boyfriend. And we didn't tell him we'd stumbled into a mystery that had been so buried in time and erased by fire, I wasn't sure it could be solved.

Hugo came downstairs to tell us, "I taught Jacob how to beatbox. It might not be his calling, though."

I rubbed Hugo's head affectionately until he squirmed away. Then we all sat down to a dinner of lamb chops and green beans almondine, finishing the meal with a *mousse au chocolat*. This dinner Jacob had made with love made me sorry I'd doubted him, and yet I doubted him still.

After dinner had been cleared away, Jacob mooched around the downstairs rooms, watching the news, taking his computer for a spin, effectively blocking the entrance to the cellar, where unread papers called out to me.

Yes, Jacob had said he would tell me about Katherine, but I wanted answers I could verify before having a chat with my Israeli commando uncle.

Harry said he had some thinking and composing to do, and after he secluded himself in the back garden, I climbed the stairs to my room. I opened a closet and found a silk nightgown and matching robe made of cerise silk. As I put it on, the silk drifted over my head and floated around my shoulders like it had been lonely for me. I got into bed and thought about Katherine and Dominick's doomed love story, and frankly, it didn't track.

I do believe it's possible to be rear-ended and not see the vehicle that struck you from behind. I believe it's possible that in the inferno that followed, other drivers had been shocked and horrified by the flames and had missed seeing the guilty driver who, after rear-ending Dominick's motorcycle, sped away.

But why had Uncle Pig threatened Dominick?

Why wasn't he more concerned for Kath's boyfriend, the other victim in this accident? Why hadn't he waited for Dominick to recover and maybe helped him pursue legal matters arising from the accident? That would have been humane. And why hadn't Dominick been allowed to contact my parents and tell them about Katherine's last days?

That might have been a comfort to us all.

Instead, we'd had Katherine's funeral without the boy who loved her. What could be sadder than that? Had Peter been at the funeral? I couldn't remember.

After our parents died, I'd caught Peter smuggling documents out of my father's office. He had said the papers belonged to Angel Pharmaceuticals and, therefore, to him.

Now I wondered if those papers were all about Katherine. Was there a connection between Katherine's drug protocols and her death?

I had to find out.

I have a track record of solving crimes, starting with the deaths of our parents and continuing from that day, so that I even get respect from the NYPD.

So I say this not as a snotty teenager, but as a proven investigator: *Uncovering the mystery of Katherine's death would be the most important investigation of my life.*

That was my last conscious thought before I dropped into a black hole of sleep.

I had to swim up from the depths of my slumber to finally understand that Jacob was knocking frantically on my door.

"Tandy! Open up. It's an emergency."

"What time is it?"

"It's late. Get dressed, Tandy. Harry is in trouble."

I bounded out of bed in my borrowed peignoir and threw open the door.

"What is it? What happened?"

"Someone is *dead*. Harry has been arrested."

25

Monsieur Morel surprised me.

I was slammed against the backseat as he floored the Mercedes, cutting through early-morning traffic and whizzing through intersections against lights, without incident or accident.

Hugo clung to me in the backseat as the car lurched and swayed and shot through the streets of Paris.

We couldn't go fast enough for me.

My heart ached for Harry. Was he terrified? Had the police already decided he was guilty of something heinous? It had happened before, to Matty when his girlfriend had been found stabbed to death. The media had played judge and jury before the trial even started.

Before I could get swamped in bad memories, Monsieur Morel braked the car outside the Commissariat de Police. Car doors flew open, and with Jacob in the lead, Hugo and I nimbly skirted a long row of bike racks and iron fencing, edging through a line of police cars at the curb.

The police station was gray brick, lit from within with a stark, bluish-gray light, looking quite ominous under the circumstances.

Jacob held the glass doors for Hugo and me, saying, "Don't worry, kids," in a way that sounded like he was worried *sick*.

The police station looked like every one I've ever seen. There were community notices on the walls and long counters around the perimeter for filling out forms. There was a bank of folding chairs in the middle and one in a corner, and another all the way at the back of the room; a desk was manned by two uniformed officers, a big clock on the wall behind their heads.

In front of the desk were two staggered lines of drunks and thieves, and also parents and loved ones making inquiries.

As I stood in the entrance taking all this in, a man approached from the edge of my vision. He was chubby, bald, and wearing jeans, a gray plaid sports jacket, and a scowl. That was when I recognized him. It was Gram Hilda's senior attorney, Monsieur Delavergne.

He shook hands with Jacob, nodded hello in the direction of Hugo and me, and then walked us to the cluster of folding chairs in the corner of the room.

Jacob asked him, "Where do things stand?"

Delavergne spoke mainly in English but stopped every now and then to look for the correct word.

"Put simply, Harry went to a party, what I would call an out-of-control bacchanal with no adults on the premises. The girl who invited him to the party, Lulu Ferrara, overdosed and died in a bathroom."

Jacob expressed his shock, then asked, "Did Harry give drugs to this girl?"

"He says not," said Delavergne, "and there are no witnesses to the contrary, but the two of them came to the party together, and that makes Harry a person of interest—at the least."

I shouted, *"Harry went with someone to a party? That's what he did? That's IT?"*

Ignoring me, Delavergne went on. "Mademoiselle Ferrara's father is deputy foreign attaché to the Italian Consulate. Obviously, Monsieur Ferrara is pulling out—how do you say?—the 'big guns.'"

Jacob said, "Big guns be damned. What are the charges

against my nephew? If he's not charged, they have to release him, isn't that true in this country?"

Delavergne said, "At present he is being held as a—"

Even as Delavergne said *"Témoin important,"* I said, "Material witness."

I knew the drill. Where I come from, material witnesses can be held for forty-eight hours, enough time to break down a hardened street thug into a sobbing baby. Harry was no hardened anything. With enough skill, a cagey cop could get him to confess to something he didn't do.

I was sweating and chilled at the same time.

I was about to start shouting again when Delavergne turned his head toward the intake desk. He said to Jacob, "One moment. I'm being called."

Delavergne went over to the desk sergeant, who took him through a side door. The door closed behind them, and a few minutes later, the sergeant returned to the desk alone.

We waited.

Hugo was crying softly. "This isn't right. Harry didn't kill *anyone.*"

I grabbed my brother and held him tight.

I said, "Jacob, do you trust Monsieur Delavergne?"

"He's a good lawyer. In fact, he's very good."

Of course I noticed that Jacob hadn't answered my question.

26

Jacob, Hugo, and I hunkered down in plastic chairs in the police station's lobby for three endless hours.

My uncle and I took turns pacing. Sometimes we spoke to each other in screaming whispers, then went dead quiet so we didn't wake Hugo, who was sleeping on the floor at our feet.

Finally, as sunlight pierced the front windows, Monsieur Delavergne came through the metal door with his arm around Harry's shoulders.

I jumped to my feet, stepping on Hugo's hand.

"Owwwwww!"

"Sorry, Hugo."

I looked at Harry coming across the room with Delavergne. Harry was free—right? He looked terrible—both weak and pale, like he'd spent the night running on a treadmill. I'm sure the all-night interrogation must have felt exactly like that. But all that mattered now was that we had him back.

Hugo called out to Harry and started running to him. Jacob and I were only steps behind. We all hugged Harry really hard, but he hardly hugged us back.

"Are you okay?" I asked. "What did they do to you?"

"I'm really mad," he said. "Does that count for anything?"

Delavergne said, "You'll be all right, *mon fils*. Jacob, you can take this young man home. There may be more questions until Monsieur Ferrara accepts the facts of his daughter's death, but right now, Harry is free."

Delavergne had fought for my brother, and he had *won*. I felt a little explosion of intense love for the man, until Delavergne said to our uncle, "Jacob, you and I have to meet. The board will have to be informed of this situation. On the other hand—they may already know."

I whipped around, looked out through the front windows, and saw a pack of people jostling for position behind the short iron fence on the median strip.

My heart, already exhausted from today's workout, sank.

The *press* had found us. *Mega*-press. And then we were out on the street with Harry.

From the insignias on their caps, jackets, and satellite vans, the reporters were French, American, German, and English, both TV and print journalists, all of them shouting.

"Harry Angel. *Harry!*"

"Harry. Over here. Look this way."

"Did you give drugs to Lulu Ferrara?"

Monsieur Delavergne, Jacob, and Monsieur Morel formed a wall of muscle, and I followed right behind them with a brother under each arm.

Harry hissed to me, "I didn't hurt anyone. You know that's the last thing I would ever do."

I said, "I know that. Who knows you better than me?"

We were only steps away from the safety of the car when Harry's knees buckled. He gasped, his eyes rolled back, and then my brother dropped to the pavement.

I screamed, *"Harry! Harry, what's wrong? Jacob, help!"*

Harry was shaking horribly, twitching and foaming as the press jumped the median strip barrier. Oh my God, what was wrong with Harry? Had he been poisoned with whatever had killed Lulu?

Was he dying?

Hugo threw himself on top of Harry, covering him as best he could, protecting him from the clicking cameras and the rolling tape. I pulled at Hugo. "Hugo, no. He has to breathe."

I heard Jacob directing Delavergne and Morel to lift Harry into the car. It was all happening too slowly.

I pushed Hugo into the backseat after Harry, then scrambled in behind him and closed the door. Harry was moaning, still shuddering and twitching.

"We've got to get to the hospital. Fast!" I shouted.

Jacob said to us, "Buckle up." And to Morel, "Let's go."

27

The American Hospital was to hospitals what the Plaza is to hotels. It was an awesome place with famous doctors and the best medical services on the Continent. And then there were the bonus amenities like Wi-Fi; gourmet meals; and hairdressers, pedicurists, and masseuses by appointment.

It was almost like a resort where you could have brain surgery and get a high-fashion haircut at the same time.

Hugo kept Harry company while Harry's doctor met with Jacob and me outside the closed door. Since Dr. West is a highly regarded cardiac surgeon and I'm a sixteen-year-old girl, needless to say, he spoke over my head.

He said to my uncle, "Harrison's symptoms: breathlessness, dizziness, and the syncope—that's fainting—the fluttering in the chest and sudden weakness—these all are indications of tachycardia. It's generally not very serious, and I've seen a lot of this in teenage boys.

"But you should know that tachycardia can be brought on by using energy drinks—either alone or as a mixer. Stimulant drugs like cocaine can also bring on tachycardia. Given that Harrison had been at a party, followed by the stress of the police interrogation, it all makes sense. I'm not concerned with the tachycardia—"

I interrupted. "So is he going to be all right?"

The doctor ignored me. "As for the arrhythmia, this is an irregular heartbeat that *can* be life threatening…"

Dr. West went on, saying that arrhythmia, or fibrillation, was potentially more serious, and that pretty much infuriated me.

Because I wasn't convinced that any of my brother's heart issues were caused by congenital defects or energy drinks mixed with booze or recreational drugs.

A different idea had occurred to me. A bad one.

I pushed open the door to Harry's hospital room. It was a big, bright corner room, furnished with a super-comfy sit-up bed and a reclining chair currently occupied by Hugo, who was enthusiastically thumbing his Nintendo 3DS.

I saw a couple of huge, ostentatious flower arrangements and a garish bouquet of metallic balloons tied to the footrail. Who had sent them? Harry had arrived just hours ago.

Behind the balloons, Harry was sitting up in bed, talking on his phone. He had good color in his face, an open laptop on his knees, and papers littering his blanket. The papers looked legal. Like contracts. In fact, my brother looked less like a heart patient and more like a whiz-kid businessman.

He held up a finger to me, the universal gesture for "just a minute," and said into the phone, "Yes, I can make it to the audition tomorrow at three. Thank you. Thank you very much."

He clicked off his phone and grinned.

"Who was that?" I asked. "What kind of audition?"

"Haven't you heard, Tandy? I'm a musical genius. I'm about to take Paris by storm."

I sat on the edge of the bed. It felt like I was in a convenience store and a live deer had wandered inside. And when that happens, you want to approach it very carefully so that it doesn't go nuts and break up the place before leaping through the plate glass window.

"Dr. West said you have heart problems, Harry. You know that?"

"I heard him. I guess maybe I did party a little too hard. But it was no big deal, Tandy. I don't know what Lulu 'ingested' because I lost sight of her the second we walked through the door. All I had was a couple of beers—"

I cut him off because he was seriously scaring me. I said, "Do not lie to me. I have to know. Are you taking the *pills* again? Are you having a reaction to our illegal, non-FDA-approved pills with whatever you 'ingested' at that party?"

"I'm not taking the pills," he said. "I stopped taking them when you did. When our supply was cut off."

"Harry, if you're lying, if you're mixing pills and other things, you could *die*."

He shook his head. Like he couldn't accept that I didn't believe him. Well, there were boxes of pills in our father's office when he died. Harry had had plenty of opportunity to stash some away for the future.

I had done it. Maybe all my brothers had, too.

Our drugs had their advantages.

Hugo looked up from his 3DS. He said to me, "He keeps them in a vitamin C bottle inside his suitcase. A big bottle."

Harry glared at Hugo, then turned an even angrier

glare on me. "I said, I'm not taking any pills, Tandy. Don't worry. The Harry you're seeing is all me. Something huge is about to happen, and I can't afford not to be one hundred percent.

"Finally, it'll be my time to shine."

28

When I peeked in on Harry that night, he was cross-legged on his bed, scrawling on music sheets, humming to himself and counting off beats on his fingers. He looked good. He didn't see me open and close his door.

Across the hall in his own room, Hugo was surrounded by pillows on the floor, intensely involved in a football game on the giant TV, shouting out to Matty, who was on Skype watching the game with him from thousands of miles away.

Meanwhile, downstairs in the dining room, Jacob was having coffee and cake with Monsieur Delavergne. After my sunburst of love for Gram Hilda's lawyer, I now had to see things as they actually were. And reality sucked.

Harry had left home without permission.

He'd gone to a wild party, where his "date" had died of an ecstasy overdose. And probably even more disgraceful—the press had videotaped Harry Angel's arrest, his release, and his fall in front of the police station. Now everything that had ever been said, filmed, or written about our family was being regurgitated for a whole new audience.

Most of our recorded history was pretty disgraceful, to say the least.

I went to the kitchen and washed the dinner dishes, soaking them in hot water and scrubbing vigorously while the meeting that might turn Harry's inheritance to crap rumbled along out of earshot. I was totally terrified for Harry.

On the other hand—and wasn't there always another hand?—I understood why Harry was rebelling.

Harry's paintings, in my humble estimation, were brilliant. He also composed music and could really, *really* play the piano.

Our parents hadn't appreciated these talents; they thought his brand of creativity was weak. Or they didn't see a financial advantage to painting and music. Or they really didn't like Harry, which was *his* opinion. He was the unloved child.

Whatever, because of Harry's epic press coverage,

reporters had learned of his debut at Carnegie Hall and that he'd written music for other musicians.

They'd figured out their angle, which was also the truth: Harry was an oppressed musical *giant*. Now there was interest in Harry, all right. Big-money interest.

I took a few swigs of cooking sherry, nearly dropping the bottle when my phone suddenly rang.

Could it be James?

I leapt for my phone, which was on the kitchen table a mile away. I grabbed it and eyeballed the caller ID.

It wasn't James.

But a thrill shot through me anyway.

I was almost as excited as if James was actually calling me. I clicked the phone, put my mouth to the speaker, and *screamed*.

29

She screamed, too.

She was Claudia Portman, aka C.P., my best friend from school—really my *only* friend from school. C.P. is a bold dresser, a loud talker, and like me, she tends to color outside the lines. I'm *her* "only," too.

When I last saw C.P. a week ago, my family was fleeing New York, probably for good. We were about to cab it down to the docks and within hours board the *Queen Mary 2* and sail to France, our future unknown. I also hadn't known until C.P. told me on the street that day that she had spent the night in Harry's room.

Why did this feel bad? I don't know, but I'd made her promise to never, under any circumstance, even if we hated each other, even if I pointed a gun at her head, tell me about having sex with my brother. *Vom*.

So I don't know anything about *that*, and I buried this tidbit under a wrinkle in my cerebral cortex and moved on.

Now—C.P. was screaming into my ear, and then she said, "Tandy! Why didn't you call me back?"

"You called?" I said. "When?"

"Yesterday. And—two *days* ago. And the day after you left me in New York—all by myself!"

I laughed loud and hard. God, it felt good to laugh from my belly, especially great because she was laughing now, too.

I gasped for air. And then I said, "Sorry, C.P. I didn't have the satellite hookup when we were on the ship, and then I was at school—no phone, and then Jacob took all our phones away, and then Harry was in the hospital—"

"Hospital? What's wrong with Harry?"

I skipped the part about his date with Lulu Ferrara—Harry could tell C.P. about *that* if he wanted to—but I did say he'd had some heart palpitations and that he was okay.

But I wasn't done. I had to backtrack to tell C.P. about Gram Hilda's "gifts and challenges."

"It's like, 'Don't disgrace the family, or bread crusts for you.' And you know, C.P., my brothers and I do tend to ruffle feathers."

C.P. laughed again and said, "I think it's still hashtag lucky bitch."

"Maybe, but I'm talking too much. What's up with you? Any new guys to fill me in on?"

"Noooooooooo, don't stop now. What happened with James? Did you ever hear from him?"

Whomp. C.P.'s question was a huge gut punch, one that just about laid me out. I swallowed a few times, took in a lot of air and let it out, and then said, "Better than hearing from James, C.P. I *saw* him."

There was more shrieking in my right ear, and this time, I held the phone away. Truth is, I didn't want to have to talk about James, and that was why I hadn't called her right away.

"You really saw him?" C.P. asked. "Oh my God. Tell me everything."

I was evasive at first, edging around the corners of the thing. Then I started talking for real, telling her almost everything—and couldn't stop until the end of the entire sick story when I found James's note on the floor of his room.

"Tell me word for word what he wrote," C.P. said, "and don't tell me you don't remember. You have a photographic memory. We both know that."

So I swallowed and then quoted the letter, including the last line James had written:

"*Don't ever doubt that I love you. And always will.*"

Those last words were like shards of glass in my throat. I started crying, and C.P. was snuffling, too, and I'd like to say that by the time I hung up the phone, I felt better.

I could *say* that.

But it would be a damned lie.

CONFESSION

I know it's hard to believe, but I loved my parents. Because even though they did heinous things to us, I'm pretty sure—no, I'm *absolutely* sure—that despite their craziness, they wanted us to become extraordinary.

They just didn't realize they were also turning us into freaks. Or maybe they believed the end justified the means.

The pills they gave me were supposed to hone and heighten my analytical mind, and at the same time, they were designed to quash pesky, distracting, irrelevant emotions.

I didn't feel much—anger, sadness, joy—and I didn't know what I was missing.

When I met James, our love pushed through what years of

experimental drugs had blocked. No wonder I was thunder-struck. To the core. This was first love of the epic kind.

Meanwhile, my mother convinced her biggest client—Royal Rampling—to invest heavily in Angel Pharmaceuticals, which was going bankrupt. It was as though a ginormous sinkhole had opened up and the family business fell through.

Mr. Rampling lost fifty million dollars because of my parents, and he had sued the Angels for every nickel.

After I'd said good-bye to C.P. on the phone, while I was washing my face and putting my clothes away, I thought about my reunion with James in Paris, the absolute best and worst twenty-four hours of my life. I remembered how he had reeled me in—only to smash my heart into subatomic particles.

I had always assumed that, like me, James was a victim of his terrible father.

Was it possible that James was not a victim? Had he set me up to hurt me as payback for what my parents had done to his family? Had he snuck into my heart under the cover of love and purposely shattered it?

Had James Rampling been my enemy all along?

FOR ALL THE LOST GIRLS IN PARIS

30

After my hilarious but emotional conversation with C.P., and my postconversation depression, the week whizzed by, drama free. No word from James. No fights at school. No trouble from Harry's heart or Gram Hilda's apparently merciful board of judgment. And no one died.

Then we had a half-day school holiday—yay!

While Harry went to a studio to practice piano and Monsieur Morel drove Jacob and Hugo to watch a soccer camp practice game, I made a call. Then I dressed in skinny pants and heels and a fierce narrow-waisted checked jacket, and I pulled my hair back in a braided band. I put on makeup, too, for the first time since the Sisters of Charity got hold of me.

I caught a cab at the taxi stand down the street, and twenty minutes and eight kilometers later, my royal-blue Fiat taxi slowed to a crawl along a charming, narrow street in Le Marais.

We stopped in front of a two-story powder-blue building with high, sparkling windows and gold letters on the awnings over the glass-and-brass front doors.

We were at the Parfumerie Bellaire, my grandmother's company and the prettiest shop I'd ever seen.

I walked through the doorway into a dazzling showroom, almost like a stage set in a theater. Clerks, not much older than me, wore colorful smocks over tights, with chunky jewelry and stylish hair fascinators. Behind the showcases, the walls were paneled with luminous photos of sunlit fields of flowers: lavender and roses and blue-eyed grass.

My grandmother had created this. This had been her passion.

I told a clerk my name, and the young woman clasped my hands in hers and said, "Monsieur Laurier is waiting for you. He asked me to bring you right in."

The laboratory behind the showroom was a bright, open space with skylights overhead, furnished with wooden tables around the perimeter and tall, narrow shelves holding flasks and vials and copper beakers. Workers in pale-blue lab coats and gold net caps used little glass pipettes to blend tiny portions of fragrant oils. Wow, the air smelled absolutely heavenly.

Monsieur Laurier came downstairs from his office on the mezzanine. He strode toward me, introduced himself, shook my hand, and then—he hugged me.

He was a very handsome man of at least seventy. How can such an old dude be so gorgeous? I can only say that he *was*.

"*Bonjour.* I'm honored to meet you, Tandy. I am so glad for the chance to show you Bellaire."

Monsieur Laurier walked me through the lab and explained that the young people at the tables had all been specially trained.

"They spent nine months learning to recognize a minimum of five hundred fragrances and must spend five more years in their apprenticeships before they can identify four thousand scents—and become a recognized 'nose' for Bellaire.

"Your grandmother was a great woman," said Monsieur Laurier. "She inspired so many people—myself included."

As we walked, Monsieur Laurier stopped at various

stations to introduce me and to place drops of fragrant oil on fabric for me to smell. I sniffed vanilla and lemongrass, ylang-ylang and musk, sandalwood and amber, and all the while Monsieur Laurier was watching me, showing me, teaching me.

And he told me, "Your grandmother was an extraordinary nose. She had a genius for creating new fragrances that we still sell today. Even now, there is no one like her."

A shadow crossed Monsieur Laurier's face. Sadness or nostalgia, and suddenly I thought I'd seen him before. Was he one of the nude men in the photos I'd found in Gram Hilda's locked attic room?

I asked, "Monsieur Laurier, how well did you know my grandmother?"

He smiled, and it was almost as if he was glad I had figured it out.

"Would it surprise you if I said I was in love with her?"

Later, when Monsieur Laurier walked me out to the taxi, he gave me a beautiful powder-blue box tied with gold ribbons.

"This is a collection of Hilda's favorite *parfums*," he said. Then he kissed me on each cheek and wished me a *bonne journée*.

I clutched the package as the driver headed toward

Gram Hilda's house. And I actually picked out one fragrance wafting through the package.

Maybe I had inherited my Gram Hilda's nose.

The fragrance was Se Souvenir de Moi.

Remember me.

31

I sat back in the rear seat of the taxi and watched the grand, timeless architecture of one of the world's great cities go by. As the cab sped along the Quai des Tuileries, the driver said to me, "By chance, do you know the car behind us?"

I turned my head and saw a black SUV.

"How long has this car been following us?" I asked.

The driver said, "I think I saw him waiting at the corner when you got into my taxi. I cannot be sure. Anyway, there he goes."

The black car sped past us on the inside lane as we went through an underpass. I couldn't see the driver or anyone in the black car, but inside the sudden deep shadow of the tunnel, I felt a chill.

Had James told me the truth when he said his father was more dangerous than I knew?

I pulled my phone from my bag and called Jacob. But my call went to voice mail—twice. And then my taxi was drawing close to home. I looked out the back window— no one was behind us. I checked out the main streets and the side streets and saw no idling cars, no men under streetlamps. I saw nothing suspicious at all.

The driver stopped at Gram Hilda's front gate, and to my tremendous relief, I saw lights on inside the house. I paid the driver and thanked him, and after entering the front garden, I trotted up the walk and turned my key in the front door.

Jacob was in the parlor.

He whipped around when he saw me, and there was something frightening in his expression.

"Tandy, I've been trying to reach you."

"What? Why?"

"Hugo is missing."

"Jacob, what do you mean?"

Jacob said, "One minute he was beside me at the soc-cer field. He said he wanted to go to the bathroom—and then—he was just gone. Monsieur Morel is looking for him all around the field. I've called the police, but he's only been gone for three hours. Not quite three hours, but he has never done this before. I have never been this frightened."

"Maybe he's with Harry?"

"Harry hasn't seen him or heard from him. Harry is on his way home now."

Jacob, who rarely panics, was panicked now. And that only made me more afraid. Had whoever was in the black SUV captured Hugo? Was my little brother a prisoner?

Jacob's Israeli accent was now so thick, it was hard to understand him.

He said something like, "Let's put our heads together, Tandy. Say he's just having a good time. That he's not in trouble. Say he's not thinking that he's giving us heart failure because he's missing. Where would he be?"

I forced myself to stop thinking about black cars and a little boy in the back with a hood over his head, hands and feet duct-taped together.

As soon as I put the fear away, a very different picture appeared in my mind. Of a confident, impetuous, no-rules-apply kid who had the strength of a grown man.

"I have an idea," I said. "I don't know if it's right or wrong, but at least it's an *idea*."

32

Having known Hugo his whole life, I had pretty good insight into what he might be thinking.

On our third night in Paris, Hugo had discovered Ladurée, a famous pastel-green-painted tea and pastry salon with seductive confections in the window on the magnificent Champs-Élysées.

We had gotten lucky that night, Hugo, Harry, Jacob, and I. There had been a table available on the first-floor terrace. We had a terrific meal, but rather than taking in the outrageously gorgeous *crème de Paris* view, we were fascinated by Hugo.

I could still see him that first time at Ladurée. My little brother gorged on dinner, then doubled down on dessert:

a dozen of the house specialty *macarons*, which are like rainbow-colored meringue Oreos stuffed with jam, cream, or chocolate.

I think that for Hugo that meal was a peak experience.

Hugo had begged to go back to Ladurée almost every night since that first time, but we were grounded most nights, and when we weren't eating Jacob's home-cooked dinners, there were other places to try. We were in *Paris*.

But Hugo had fallen hard for Ladurée.

Only minutes after Jacob called him, Harry's arrival at Ladurée coincided with ours and the three of us made a plan. Jacob interviewed the maître d' and pressed some bills into his hand, and then we spread out and searched the establishment for a kid with chocolate on his face.

I took the ground floor, Harry frisked the five rooms upstairs, and Jacob checked out the kitchen and all the bathroom stalls.

We met up again in the main salon—empty-handed.

"He'll *be* here," I said. "I just know it."

No one believed me, but still, we took seats at a table in the front room, and Jacob called Monsieur Morel, asking him to go to the house and wait there in case Hugo came home.

I called the waiter to our table.

"We need a platter of chocolate croissants, *s'il vous*

plaît," I said, pointing to a heap of them in the display case. "And pots of hot chocolate. *Pots.*"

I had no appetite, but ordering chocolate was like baiting a trap for Hugo. When the croissants were just a buttery smear on the plate and Hugo still hadn't arrived, my fluttering uncertainty was growing into full-fledged panic. Harry leaned forward and said, "You can't be right all the time, sis."

"I hate to do it," Jacob said, "but we have waited long enough. We must go to our nuclear option. I'm calling Monsieur Delavergne. He may be able to fire up the police." He picked up his phone and began pressing the dreaded numbers.

It was the right thing to do, but I felt that once our lawyers were in play, we were lost. This would be the last straw for them. I felt a tightness in my throat and a watery feeling in my guts. I was one second from a weepy public meltdown; then I saw a kid in a red All Saints lacrosse shirt rounding the confections counter.

I jumped up, grabbed Hugo roughly by the arm, and angrily demanded, "*Hugo!* Are you all right? What's wrong with you? Where the hell were you?"

God, I was mad.

Hugo trudged ahead of me toward the table, looking defiant. Which was totally nuts.

"I went to the bathroom," he said. "And then I went to the locker room to look around, and when I came out, Uncle Jacob, you were gone."

"I was looking for *you*," said Jacob. "Why didn't you call me? Why didn't you wait?"

"I lost my phone, so I looked for Monsieur Morel. And then this black SUV zoomed toward me. It was scary… like it was waiting for me. I thought it was going to run me *down*."

I wanted to throw up. Another black car. Waiting, zooming. I reached for my little brother, but he didn't want comforting.

"Wait, so let me tell you. I ran into a bookstore, and when I went out the back door, the black car was gone."

Hugo went on, "And then I got into the Métro and here I am. You should stop thinking of me as an ordinary little kid, you know? I can get around really well."

In the speechless silence around the table, Hugo eyed the empty plates.

"You guys were hungry, too? I need *macarons*, really bad."

Jacob said, "Two words, Hugo."

"Let me guess. 'You're grounded.' "

"Correct." Jacob signaled to the waiter.

"You're so predictable," said Hugo.

"Yes, and predictability is exactly what you kids need in your lives right now. Tandy, good call."

Then our uncle put down his phone and closed his eyes. Jacob might have been an Israeli commando, but it was obvious that babysitting the Angels was one of the harder missions he'd ever undertaken.

33

It was late, sometime after one.

The house was dark except for the small room tucked inside the basement. No light escaped that dungeon, and yeah, Jacob wouldn't like me being there. But in my not-so-humble opinion, my needs were greater than his.

Katherine was *my* sister. And I was going to go through her boxes. I had the right to do it.

The last few weeks had thrown out too many questions without answers.

The mystery that nagged me night and day was Katherine's death in South Africa. I hadn't questioned what I'd been told until Dominick said Uncle Peter had threatened his life.

Why had Peter done that?

What didn't Peter want anyone to know?

The threat against Dominick was just one in a pattern of threats.

Besides Uncle Peter's, there were Royal Rampling's multiple warnings and the ongoing danger James had warned me about.

And now I was questioning everything.

I reached into a box and lifted out a large unsealed envelope that was filled with loose documents of all sizes and colors. I spilled the enclosed papers onto the monastery table and was sorting them out with my fingertips when a letter with a drawing on the bottom grabbed my attention and wouldn't let go.

I recognized that letter. Because I had written it to Katherine. In my clear genius-in-training handwriting, I had written:

Dear Kath,

I hope you find the diamonds you want to make into a necklace that will light up a room. And if you find smaller diamonds that light up a smaller room and look good on a ten-year-old, please bring them home to me.

Love, your very adorable sister,
The Amazing Tandoo

At the bottom of the page, I'd drawn a picture of myself and Kath with marking pens, both of us wearing blue dresses and diamond necklaces with rays shooting out of the stones, both of us with big dopey smiles.

I had loved Katherine so much. The way Hugo adores Matty. Wanted to wear her clothes. Wanted her approval. Wanted to grow up to be just like her. And damn, I teared up again.

This happened too often since I stopped taking the pills. I'm amazed at the strength of my feelings and totally scared of them at the same time. I'm just not prepared for floods of emotions that I can't control. I'm like an ice girl who has just come in from the cold.

This is what I was thinking when the door behind me opened. I screamed and jumped back—but it was only Hugo. He'd always been good at finding hiding spots.

"What are you doing?" he asked me.

After I caught my breath and was pretty sure I wasn't going to have a heart attack, I showed Hugo the letter I'd written to Katherine.

"Do you remember her, Hugo?"

"Sure," he said. "She used to carry me around the apartment. She smelled good. Hey. You smell like her. Don't you?"

"Yeah. Good nose, bro."

I laughed, and we hugged.

"I'm sorry I scared you today," he said. "I was so freaked out myself, I didn't think about you guys worrying that I'd been killed or something. This is my formal apology, Tandy."

He looked so serious, I cracked up.

"I accept," I said.

"O-kayyyy. I love you, you know?"

"I love you, too, you little monster. Now, go back to bed. Please? I'm working."

34

I closed the door behind Hugo and went back to the box I'd been digging around in before he jump-started my nervous system. I was still winded from that.

As I sorted through miscellaneous Katherine-related documents, I wondered again: Who had collected Katherine's papers and lab reports? Who had locked them in a basement-within-a-basement in a place where no one lived?

Who had hired a detective to watch her, and why?

I made small piles of papers, some from MIT, where Katherine would have gone to college. There were documents from passport offices in France, South Africa, and New York.

I was about to close the box, which seemed to be filled

with personal documents of little importance, when my hand fell on a short stack of cream-colored stationery— just the notepaper, not the envelopes. The paper was heavy, and the dates written in the top left-hand corner were just the day of the week, not the month or year.

I unfolded one of the notes, and to be honest, from the moment I read *My dearest Katherine*, I got a queasy feeling. I had no business reading my sister's mail.

But it was too late to stop now, right?

The letter was written in blue fine-point marker and read:

Thursday

My dearest Katherine,
I know you as well as I know my own face, feel your feelings as if they were my own. I'm sorry I've upset you. I didn't mean to do it. I suggest we meet again so we can talk everything over. I think we owe each other that.

Fondest love,
P.

What was this? A love letter? Who was P.? Or was that really the initial *D*? The writing was just ambiguous enough that I couldn't be sure.

So I had to read the next letter in the stack. Wouldn't anyone in my position do the same?

The second letter looked and sounded similar to the first:

Monday

My dearest Katherine,
Seeing you, today, well…Thank you for seeing me.
You are the most precious person on earth to me.
And I know some people would say it's wrong, but
I think we both know that when it's right, only the
people involved have the right to say.

All my love,
P.

Yes, it was definitely a *P.*

I opened a third letter and a fourth, and in this last letter, I saw something that made me want to throw up. P. wrote,

I've enclosed your ticket, my Angel. I'll meet you in
Cape Town. And I promise you, this time will be
special and will reveal the future.

All my love,
P.

The ticket was in the envelope, Cape Town to New York. One way. It hadn't been used, but of course, Katherine hadn't left Cape Town. And the name of the person who paid for the ticket—I had to read the typing several times before my brain would accept the name Peter Angel.

Uncle Peter. Our father's *brother.*

I felt the familiar stirrings of revulsion when I thought of Peter, especially as I recalled when he was in our apartment at the same time as Katherine. And that after our parents died and Uncle Peter was our guardian for a short while, he had moved into Katherine's room, used her desk, slept in her bed.

We all hated that. We all hated *him.*

Had he forced himself on Katherine? Had he raped her? Did he have a sick fascination with her that she didn't return? Or—please don't let it be true—did she have feelings for him, too? No. He was pleading with her. She had to have rejected him.

I pocketed the letters from Peter. If anyone confronted me about going into the boxes, I'd shove Uncle Peter's love letters in their face.

Another mystery had been added to my list, and more questions without answers.

Was Peter angry that Katherine had run off with a lover?

Was that why he had threatened Dominick's life?

As a person who knew the pain of heartbreak, I wondered if Uncle Peter had been so thoroughly hurt by Katherine's rejection that he had engineered her death.

It was a crazy theory. But when Angels are involved, crazy is almost *normal*.

CONFESSION

As I tore through the cartons, I whispered out loud to my poor dead sister.

"Kath, it's me.

"I think you left these boxes—for me. I'm here now. I'm reading. I'm learning. I'm using the best of my analytical abilities. I'm going to figure out what happened to you. And if your death wasn't accidental, someone will pay. So help me.

"I mean that literally. Please help me.

"By the way, I love and miss you.

"And I'm still the Amazing Tandoo."

There were a million papers I hadn't looked through, but I was determined. I was going to pass my eyes over every document in this room tonight, and if there were answers in these boxes, I would find them.

I swore on my love for Katherine.

35

So. Clearly there was information in these heavy cartons, *plenty* of it. If I wanted to understand what had been done to all five of the Angel kids, I had to dive into the hard stuff—and I was way ready. I especially wanted to know more about our uncle Peter's role in the destruction of our family.

I attacked the docs by sorting them into categories, then subcategories. Hours passed, and I was in the *zone*. I refused to be sidetracked by fatigue or ghosts or ricocheting random thoughts.

After reading through the first huge stack of Angel Pharmaceuticals memoranda and lab reports, I checked my phone. It was after four AM. In a few hours, my family would start moving around upstairs, and someone would surely look for me.

I had to read *faster*.

I plowed through the next pile of documents, then pulled the third stack of papers off the table and sat on the floor with my back against the cold stone wall.

I fastened my attention on a memo to my dad from Uncle Peter, when they were both senior partners at Angel Pharmaceuticals.

The body of the memo read, "Mal. All the reports on nootropics are here. Your conclusion is required by the end of the month. P."

The table of contents in the attached file listed nootropics, including antidepressants, also hormones, brain cell protectors, and stimulants—my *God*.

My parents had given this stuff to us as *vitamins*.

"*Don't forget to take your vitamins, Tandoori.*"

"*I already took them, Dad.*"

And then I moved on to even scarier stuff: letters and memos to Uncle Peter from *government intelligence agencies* asking about the "K. Angel Experiment."

Katherine.

Some of the letters were from the CIA, but there were cryptic queries from spy agencies in Russia, France, Japan. And Israel.

Government interest in my sister was shocking and hideous, and it also made me wonder if this high-grade secret intelligence interest was why Jacob had been drawn back into the Angel family web.

I got to my feet and dug around in the very first box I had opened days ago, and found Katherine's chart. You didn't have to be a genius to see that the experiments on Katherine had gone way too far, too fast. If drugs had done this for her, I could see the applications for military use. And if there was money to be made, it would be very *big* money. My parents and uncle would have been all for that.

But what if Katherine, with her monumental IQ, had figured this out?

What if she hadn't liked being a lab animal and a business model combined? What if there had been bad side effects that my father and Peter had ignored, and she wanted to quit? And what if her side trip to Paris when she was on her way to South Africa had been one small act of rebellion, and part of a bigger plan?

Had Katherine's independence freaked someone out? Had that someone been afraid she might go over to an enemy? Was that why private investigators had been called in?

What if Katherine hid these boxes in Gram Hilda's house in case something happened to her?

I imagined too many reasons why someone might have targeted Katherine for death. I was afraid I might be on the verge of learning something horrible and too close to home.

I was panting hard enough to be heard upstairs, so I rolled up the chart, grabbed two handfuls of incriminating papers, and left the basement room.

It was time to talk to Jacob.

36

I found Jacob brewing coffee in the kitchen.

He turned, smiled, and said, "A little early for you, isn't it, Tandy?"

I put a fat stack of papers on the table, including Katherine's chart, which I unrolled and flattened out, holding down the corners with salt and pepper shakers and a couple of trivets.

I said, "I'm pretty smart, you know, Jacob? Some would say smarter than ninety-nine point nine percent of my peers."

"I don't doubt that," he said. "Is your intelligence in dispute?"

He poured two oversized mugs of coffee and brought

them to the table. He slid one over to me and pulled out a kitchen chair for himself.

Then he said, "I'm pretty sure I told you those boxes were off-limits."

"Well," I said, "as Katherine's sister, I think my rights to her stuff override your rights."

"My fault for not locking them up," Jacob muttered to himself.

I continued, "I've been in the basement for about eight hours, Jacob, and I've found some very scary shit.

"I found documents, lab reports, spy agency inquiries, and in-house memos between Peter and Malcolm proving that Angel Pharma was experimenting with nootropics, brain-enhancing drugs, as well as mood-altering drugs and strength and speed enhancers."

Jacob stirred his coffee but said nothing. I went on.

"Let's look at Katherine's official chart, okay? In one year, Katherine's IQ zoomed from a pretty brilliant one hundred thirty-three to an astonishing one hundred eighty *plus*.

"Correct me if I'm off the wall here, but an IQ boost of more than forty-five points in the course of a year has never been achieved in recorded history."

"You think Katherine was given drugs to boost her intelligence," said Jacob. He didn't sound surprised.

"You got it," I said. His flat demeanor was maddening. I stabbed the chart with my finger.

"Here's a similar trend line in four other categories: physical strength, linguistics, math, and resistance to pain."

Jacob said, "I see that."

He got up, grabbed a baguette and a tub of butter from the counter, and brought them over to the table.

I continued my very focused rant.

"This strength drug. MusX. Matty took that. It's for increasing muscle mass. Here, at the beginning of the year, Katherine could bench-press two hundred pounds. Not bad for a female high school senior with a small bone structure.

"One year later, Katherine could press four hundred forty pounds. That's about four times her weight and probably an Olympic record. Shall I go on, Uncle?"

"I've seen this chart, you know."

"So you understand, then, that MusX is an untraceable synthetic steroid made in Angel Pharma labs. This drug, plus the brain drugs, and the strength and no-pain drugs, dumbed down to commercial strength, would be pretty valuable in drugstores. But in the *full*-strength form, in the hands of military agencies, it would be *priceless*. And I can back that up, too," I said to my uncle, patting the raft of memos from spy agencies in four countries.

"Maybe Katherine ran off. Maybe it was too dangerous to Angel Pharma for Katherine to be on the loose. What happened to Katherine, Jacob? Who killed my sister and why?"

"You think that, Tandy? That she was murdered?"

"It sure looks that way to me."

Jacob shook his head. "Katherine wasn't murdered. She was killed in a collision with a bus. As for the drugs, I'll tell you what I know, but not now. It's a long story. And right now, you have to get ready for school."

I said, "After what I've just said, you're going to talk to me about *school*?"

He said, "Damned right."

I yelled and screamed like a wild animal. I threw my coffee cup hard against the wall, where it totally shattered.

Unruffled, Jacob said, "That's enough. Clean that up. And get dressed."

Then he left the kitchen.

I felt good about throwing the mug for about a second; then I felt like a drunken football player and a total idiot. I mean, throwing china is a true symbol of powerlessness.

I wiped down the wall and put the shards of the cup in

the trash. Then I grabbed the chart and other stuff and marched up to my room. I wondered if Jacob was telling me the truth about Katherine's death. He didn't seem to be lying, but experience has taught me that I can't trust any adult in my family.

Like Jacob.

Enough said.

37

I dressed in my school uniform. Which I now freaking hated. Itchy knee-highs and ugly flat shoes. No makeup. At all. Were these dowdy mouse clothes really necessary?

I was properly attired and backpack-ready when Monsieur Morel pulled up to our front gate. Not much later, I was at my desk on time, and it's a tribute to my earlier education that I was sufficiently prepared without having studied. But I was exhausted from lack of sleep. I was also heartsick and paranoid.

The pills I'd once taken had protected me from depression, but now I was nakedly vulnerable to bottomless despair and the effects of what's commonly called "birds coming home to roost."

The birds were black shadows over my past, present, and future: my parents' deaths and Katherine's, along with the constant virtual threat of Royal Rampling, who'd made every black SUV seem like a messenger from hell.

The biggest, blackest bird was the unknown.

What was going to happen to the orphaned Angels? I was still a *kid*. How was I supposed to cope with things that were so out of my control?

No, really. How?

As I wallowed in my private downward spiral, I remembered a beautiful black lacquered box my dad had given me, saying it had once belonged to Gram Hilda. The box was inlaid with mother-of-pearl flowers on the outside and had velvet-lined compartments inside, in which I kept my very special high-potency, candy-colored pills.

A black pill and a pink gelcap would put an end to these horrid sinking feelings. I fantasized about taking one.

When school was over for the day, Harry took off for his new studio and Morel dropped me at home before driving Jacob and Hugo to soccer camp. I watched the taillights of the Mercedes round the corner, then went upstairs to my room.

I found the black lacquered box in the corner of my suitcase. It looked like a jewelry box, and it had probably been used as such by Gram Hilda. Inside the box was an array of Lazr and HiQ and, especially seductive, the pink gelcaps I knew as Num. Num could take me to a crisp, clean place where there was no fear, no pain, no anxiety. It was beautiful there.

I picked up the ten remaining Num capsules and held them in my hand, rolling them back and forth in the cup of my palm. And then I dumped them back into their compartment and slammed down the lid of the box.

Didn't I *want* to have normal human emotions?

Or had my parents been right when they'd told me emotions were a useless distraction?

I knew I should take the pills to the bathroom and flush them down into the famous sewers of Paris. But I couldn't quite do it. I put the box back in my suitcase and went downstairs.

After a particularly awkward Jacob-made dinner of watery quiche, canned peas, and grapes, I returned to my room and opened my laptop.

I had letters to write. It was damned well about time.

CONFESSION

So my mother and father had been pretty much my entire world before I met James. They made the rules, handed out the Grande Gongos and the Big Chops, and jacked us up with illegal drugs. And then they died.

The evidence suggests that they drugged us to keep us on track to future success. But how had they ever thought we could survive in the world without the full use of our hearts?

I say I'd loved them, but was I capable of that?

Without overthinking, I wrote a letter to them on my laptop, letting the words flow from my fingertips:

Dear Mother and Father,
I have a few questions.

Mother, you know I admired you. But I don't understand. Didn't you want me to fall in love? Didn't you want me to get married and have someone love me as much as Malcolm loved you?

Father, I wanted to be just like you. I followed you around and tried to learn everything you knew, because I thought you were the smartest man ever. So how could you use your children as lab animals? You couldn't have known the long-term effects of those drugs. We still don't know.

Did you know what really happened to Katherine? Do you know who killed her?

And here's the big question for both of you, the one I really hate to ask: Did you love any of your children, really love us?

Your daughter,
Tandy

I felt sorry for myself, sure. And after the tears stopped leaking out of my eyes, I hit the delete key. A window popped up and asked, *Are you sure you want to delete this e-mail?*

Yes. I'm sure.

I turned off the light next to the bed, but I couldn't stop thinking.

I don't think I slept at all.

38

Overnight, my somber bottom-of-the-sea depression morphed into the foulest possible anger. Like a gathering squall about to break over a small island in the middle of the ocean.

I glared and grunted at breakfast, then got into the front seat of the house chariot with Monsieur Morel so I didn't have to talk to anyone. When we disembarked fifteen minutes later at the convent school, I barked at Harry for walking on my heels.

He said, "Shut up, Tandy. Meet me at lunch. I've got something to tell you."

At noon, I made it to the lunchroom before Harry did.

The Sisters of Charity didn't have the kind of cafeteria

we have in schools at home. Tables lined a windowed wall and were laden with baskets of bread, a kettle of clear soup, fruit and cheese, and compotes of pudding. I was suddenly ravenous.

When Harry showed up, we loaded up our trays and walked together to an empty table.

I was fully aware of the kids around us, with their racket reverberating through the big hall. They seemed so young to me, so innocent. Nothing like me or my brothers.

I dipped bread in my soup, and as I ate, I kept my eyes on Harry.

His face was flushed. His hair was wild. His glasses were seesawing on the bridge of his nose. He was elated and hyper, which stirred up my darker-than-dark mood.

Harry said, "You okay, Tandy?"

"Me? I'm fine."

"Oh, right," he said. "What do you call that toxic cloud right over your head?"

"I'm *fine*."

"You're lying. You know it. I know it. And you *know*—"

"So *what* do you want to tell me, Harry? I'm not asking you again."

"I'm not going to *tell* you," he said, "but I'm definitely going to *show* you. After school."

I was this close to losing it, but my brother was on fire,

and whatever had lit that little blaze, I had to go with it. I really couldn't let him down.

With permission from Jacob, Monsieur Morel dropped Harry and me off at a tram that took us to Suresnes, a western suburb of Paris. Harry was still being a jerk, giggling, whistling through his teeth, as we walked to an address on Rue Honoré d'Estienne d'Orves.

I followed my brother up a couple of steps to an unmarked door that had been painted an attractive marine blue. He pressed an intercom button and said his name into the grille.

The door opened with a loud double *click*.

What the hell?

"Harry, where are we? Is this your studio?"

"Brace yourself, Tandy. As they used to say when the Beatles walked out onstage, your mind is about to be blown."

Harry was one of the few kids in our generation who could get away with familiar references to the Beatles.

But then, Harry was named for George Harrison.

39

The mysterious blue door opened into a long, chilly hallway with awards and photos of recording superstars from several continents jam-packing the walls.

I recognized almost all the names and faces: CeeLo Green, Flo Rida, Celine Dion, Meshell Ndegeocello, Zazie, Adele, Selah Sue, and Sens Unik. And there were others, too many to count. I thought I could feel a vibration in those walls. But then, I was kind of a human tuning fork today.

I could feel everything, especially total awe that I was standing in a gallery of all-stars—and they had all probably come through the hallway where Harry and I were walking now.

I looked up as a door opened at the end of the hall and a tall man in black with dreadlocks and sunglasses came out.

"Heyyyyy, Harry."

Then he opened his arms and wrapped Harry in a huge hug, rocked him a little bit, and said, "How ya doing, muh man? You ready to show your stuff?"

Harry grinned and gripped the man's hand before turning to me. "Tandy, this is my agent, Michael Pogue. Michael, this is my twin sister, Tandy."

Agent? Mystified, I shook hands with Monsieur Pogue, who said, "*Enchanté*, Tan-deee. Very wonderful to meet you on Harrison's big, perhaps life-changing, day. Come in, come in. Meet some good people."

Harry and I followed Pogue into the "mix room" and were introduced to three men arranged in comfy chairs around a plank coffee table. They were all wearing sharp business suits and had good haircuts, and one had an interesting sculpted beard. They were talking to one another, but when Harry and I came in, they all stood up. Each gripped Harry's hand and clapped him on the back.

I could see curiosity in their faces. And naked hope.

I was also introduced. I was an afterthought, but I didn't care. These men were all here for Harry.

I switched my attention to the wall-to-wall console at the front of the mix room, with its hundreds of sliding levers and dials. When the two men sitting at the controls swiveled around, I recognized them as the famous producers and recording engineers Yves Creole and Winter Knight. They were the brains and the engine of this first-class international chain of mix rooms called the Smart Blue Door.

They shook my hand—well, actually, Mr. Knight took both my hands in his and mumbled praise for "the great Harry."

This was a huge moment for Harry, and I was so glad to be there for it. I watched him step through the door to the "live room." I could see him and the entire studio through the window in front of the mixing console.

Harry took his seat at right angles to a Fender Rhodes piano and a Hammond B-3 organ, both of which had been set up just for him.

Sitting behind the drums was a thin, balding man wearing denim and checkered black-and-white eyeglass frames that had been tattooed onto his face. He began speaking earnestly to my brother, who looked both younger and older than his sixteen years.

Monsieur Pogue led me to a seat with a view, saying, "Tandy, I know you've heard Harry play many times, but do you know the new piece he played for us yesterday? He calls it 'Montmartre.'"

Monsieur Creole had put on his headset and was speaking through his microphone to Harry and the percussionist. No one else spoke, not even the important-looking men sitting around me.

All eyes were fixed on my brother.

And then, looking right at me, Harry leaned into the microphone and said, "I wrote this for my sister Katherine. Actually, it's for all the lost girls in Paris."

40

There was a hush in both rooms.

Then Harry put his left hand on the keyboard of the Fender Rhodes piano, placed his right hand on the Hammond B-3 organ, and began to play.

From the first notes, I knew that Harry had the "it" factor, the rare and genuine real genius thing. This music of his was entirely original and entirely Harry, but with some new quality I'd never heard before.

No one had.

I rubbed my arms from the chill of witnessing his greatness unfold. But still, I listened with a critical ear to the introductory chords from the piano as they set the stage for a series of arpeggios—broken chords where the notes in a chord are played one at a time within one octave.

And somehow, tucked beneath the chords and arpeggios, Harry's melody slowly came alive.

Oh my God, Harry. How did you do this in two days?

The melody was quiet, haunting in a sweet and beautiful way.

Sometimes, while he played, Harry seemed to be missing, lost in the folds of his mind. At other times, he swiveled on his seat to play two-handed on one or the other instrument while his drummer kept time on the skins. That was when Harry smiled. After all he'd been through, he was happy.

More than happy.

He was transported to a magical place he'd created on his own, and now the music itself was filling me up.

I *felt* Paris in his music. I *heard* Paris. I *saw* in the chords the grand stone buildings flanking the sumptuous boulevards while the arpeggios signaled the action: the musical embodiment of people and taxis dashing and darting about.

But I couldn't ignore a sadness in the chords that made me think of Katherine. Of loving her, of the giant void she'd left and the tragedy that she only got to live for sixteen years.

And to tell the truth, I didn't want to go there.

If I'd given in to that feeling, I might have had a really

ugly cry, and I couldn't do that to my brother. Just as I was biting my lip to hold back the tears, here came Harry's delightful dancing notes, like bursts of hope and optimism that also reminded me of the Katherine I'd known and loved so much.

My sister.

And it occurred to me that Harry was also reaching into both sides of himself in this piece. Showing the sadness and the rising light. To be able to write something this strong from the heart, to be able to convey it in music, was Harry's gift in full. And it was a gift to everyone who was hearing him play.

I looked at the men sitting around me, as well as the seasoned pros at the console; they all looked as moved as I was, and more—as though they'd been truly swept away. One of the men wiped tears from his eyes with the back of his hand. Another lay back with his eyes closed and his arms opened, taking in the sound of the music entirely.

When Harry took his fingers from the keys, the live room filled with praise from the recording execs, who couldn't wait to tell my brother what I knew he'd been waiting to hear forever.

"Harry, you're *fantastic*. That's seriously good stuff, man!"

Monsieur Pogue came over to me.

He said, "You must be so proud. We think your brother has got something—I have to say—unique."

I looked into Monsieur Pogue's face and was afraid to speak. I nodded, and Monsieur Pogue saw the magnitude of what I was feeling. He put his arms out and hugged me.

He then joined the others in the live room, but I stood outside the glass and watched Harry's triumph. I could still hear the melody of his portrait of Katherine.

Harry hadn't been allowed to go to his friend Lulu's funeral. And so I wondered if Lulu, like Katherine, had been one of those lost girls of Paris.

Maybe I was one of them, too.

41

We weren't very graceful as we stumbled down the stairs to the street. We were whooping and yelling and my arms were around Harry's neck and I was jumping up and down and squealing like a groupie, telling him how freaking *great* he was, *monster* great. When just at the edge of my vision, I saw a black SUV down at the corner of the block.

"Harry!" I shouted, turning him around so he could see what I saw. *"It's that car."*

The headlights came on, and the car began to move off the curb. It was coming straight toward us. Again I screamed, "Harry!" I ran back to the Smart Blue Door and jammed down all the intercom buttons with the flat of my hand.

Harry was tugging at me. "Tandy, no. That's a *limo*."

By then the limo had cruised up to the curb and stopped. A man in a black jacket and chauffeur's cap stepped out and opened the rear door for us. That's when I saw the discreet Smart Blue Door logo on the car's door. Yeah, I felt like a complete and total fool.

Harry spoke into the building's intercom.

"Sorry, Michael. No, everything's fine. Talk to you soon."

We got into the limo, and Harry told the driver our address. Then he fell back against the seat.

"So this was maybe the best hour of my life."

"I don't have enough *words* to describe what it was like hearing you. But we can just start with *a-maz-ing*."

He *was* amazing, but was it within the human high-genius range of amazing? *Or was it something else?*

I took Harry's hand and asked once more. "You have to tell me the truth, Harry. Are you using the pills again? *Are you? Harry? The truth.*"

"Tandy? I've told you the truth. Don't ever ask me again."

"I didn't mean to insult you, bro. I'm afraid, and I have good reason to be afraid."

I looked at the back of our driver's neck through the Plexiglas transom. I flipped the switch to shut off all communication between the front and back compartments.

And still, I spoke in a murmur.

42

"Get ready," *I said softly to my twin.* "I have to drop some bombs. I went through the rest of the papers in the basement and found *love letters* from Uncle Peter to Kath."

Harry drew back. My gentle brother looked shocked and disgusted and completely *horrified*.

"Are you *kidding* me?"

"I have the letters. You can read them yourself."

"No freaking way. Kath wasn't just sixteen to his what—forty? She was his blood relative! Uncle Pig is a perv. I've hated him my whole life. I really want to throw the hell up." Harry buzzed down the window and let air blow over his face for a while.

I wasn't finished. I had to confess to Harry what I'd *done*.

"Last night," I said. "I was feeling *too much*, Harry. Like I was lying on train tracks while a hundred-car train rolled over me. So I took Num."

"Ha!" Harry shouted. "So that's why you keep accusing me of using the pills. Because *you*'ve done it."

"I made a mistake. All Num did was make me process every dark feeling even *faster*. I need to slow this bullet train down, Harry. For some very good reasons, I think you should do the same."

43

Once we were home, I turned up the oven to "roast," rubbed spices all over some chicken, put the bird into the oven, and set the timer. I snapped some beans like they'd done something mean to me. I chopped some fresh fruit with the same attitude, splashed peach brandy over it, covered the bowl with a damp cloth, and stashed it in our immense, triple-wide fridge.

After that, I set up a plate of cheese and crackers and cornichons and capers and took all of it to the media room, where Jacob and Hugo were watching one of the Bourne sagas.

"Uncle Jake. Please mind the chicken. I've got homework."

"Very good," he said. "Thanks, Tandy."

I went upstairs and locked my door. I opened my laptop and looked up news articles about Angel Pharmaceuticals. I easily found the whole sordid story of the bankruptcy of my mother's hedge fund, the collapse of Angel Pharma, and about a hundred links to articles about my parents' deaths and every putrid thing that had spilled from that.

I didn't need to read any more about the New York justice system and what my brothers and I had been through and somehow survived. But I did open every link to Peter Angel.

I reacquainted myself with his medical degree in pathology from Cornell, his early training at Pfizer, and a discovery he'd made in his thirties for a drug that relieved pain in patients with stomach cancer.

Then he'd gotten funding—no specifics on that— and started Angel Pharmaceuticals with his younger brother, my father, who was a statistician with a degree in pharmacology.

Everything else I found on Peter Angel was social. Namely, his bachelorhood, his famous dinner parties, his theatergoing and philanthropy. Pictures of him showed his characteristic flyaway hair and loud, expensive suits. Close-ups on his narrow, piggy eyes. One photo was taken at an after-theater dinner party at the Palm.

That photo at the Palm was a wide shot in a packed and narrow room. The light was golden, and I recognized the caricatures of celebrities on the walls and the giant slabs of steak in front of the diners.

But my eyes locked on something else.

There was a man sitting at the table behind Peter, someone I *almost* recognized. I read the caption under the photo. The name jumped out at me like a mugger in an alley. And there it was, another connection between Uncle Peter and our family enemy, my enemy in particular.

The man sitting at the table behind my uncle Peter was Royal Rampling.

I *stared at the photograph that* linked my uncle Peter and Royal Rampling, and I felt another mood come over me. A *bad* mood. Paranoia.

I reflected on that super-romantic night in the Hamptons when James and I were, without warning, nailed to the dunes by blinding headlights, then snatched and separated, each of us screaming the other's name.

When I woke up—or more likely, regained consciousness—it was daylight. The van that had taken me was parked in the semicircular driveway of a sterile white building I later learned was a mental institution. I was dragged from the van, and for weeks after that, I was treated with talk, drug, and electric-shock therapy that together practically rewired my brain.

I forgot about James. Forgot I ever knew him.

And I forgot the faces of the men in the van.

Suddenly, a new memory crept into my brain…one that I hadn't recalled before.

I remembered a man who stood by and watched as I was wrestled into the building, just after the hood was taken off my head. I saw his features now with a clarity I could hardly believe. I saw the messy ginger hair, got a glimpse of narrow, colorless eyes. It was my uncle Peter. *Damn* him.

It wasn't paranoia if my uncle Peter had his fingers in the pie. Make that a hand. No, make that both hands, and maybe he'd even *masterminded* the whole criminal kidnapping affair for my parents.

That frightening thought only made me question Peter's older brother more, the brother Peter had called in to watch over the Angel kids.

Yes. Uncle Peter had hired Jacob.

True, Jacob had put us back together and practically hand-carried us to our grandmother's house and our inheritance.

But why had Peter turned us over to Jacob? Because

he couldn't be bothered being our guardian? Or because Jacob was an undercover agent?

More questions without answers.

I got up from my computer, pushed a slipper chair across the floor, and wedged its back under the doorknob. I double-checked the locks on the windows and drew the curtains. When I was sure no one could get in, I got into bed and opened my laptop.

I had a letter in mind. I addressed it to my uncle Peter.

CONFESSION

I couldn't write the word Dear in front of his name. I didn't even want to call him my uncle. He wasn't family to me anymore.

I hated him more than anyone I'd ever known, and that put him at the top of a list of supremely heinous people.

Peter had not just been a saboteur and a dark presence to all of us because he could get away with it; he had sunk below my lowest expectations when he wrote those pervy letters to Katherine.

The letters were apologetic.

What had Peter done to Katherine when he *wasn't* writing to her? I wrote:

Peter,
I read what you wrote to Katherine, and it made me sick.
How could you have designs on a child? I have a sickening

feeling that I don't know even a fraction of the evil you have done. You're a psychopath. A real-life monster.

Be warned, I'm onto you. I'm investigating you, and when I uncover your criminal activities, I will take action.

Tandoori Angel

I had Peter's e-mail address. I could have easily sent this bomb right to his in-box, but I didn't do it.

I had two reasons.

One, all he would do was laugh.

Two, I didn't want to tip him off. If Peter had anything to do with Katherine's death, I wanted to nail him.

I hit the delete key.

Of course, the program asked, *Are you sure you want to delete this e-mail?*

Yes. I'm sure. Damn him.

Delete.

45

I woke to the sound of Jacob screaming.

Jacob never screams.

I realized I had fallen asleep, fully clothed, with my shoes on, so I ran downstairs in yesterday's school clothes to the sound of Uncle Jake shouting at the top of his lungs in his guttural mother tongue.

I didn't know what time it was, only that it was dark outside the windows and that a pool of light filled the downstairs area at the bottom of the staircase.

When I reached the landing above the foyer, I saw a bunch of kids, maybe ten of them, most a few years older than Harry and me. They were in various stages of dress and undress, and from the lazy way they were stumbling around, I was sure they were stoned.

The front door was open, and Jacob was holding a boy by the shoulder with one hand and by the waistband with the other and shoving him out the door.

Other kids, heavily inked and pierced and made up, music types maybe, grumbled and shouted at Jacob and collected their possessions at their leisure, as Jacob ranted—at Harry.

I got to the ground floor in a hurry. The parlor was trashed. Bottles and bongs and items of clothing were everywhere. The leather furniture was wet and stained. Someone had puked on the carpet.

Harry was sweaty and shirtless—no tattoos, thank God—but he looked wild-eyed, and he was grinning. He was saying, "Jacob, you're making a big deal out of nothing."

Picture Jacob's intense glare as he tried not to smack Harry for talking back.

"Nothing? You didn't have permission to bring people here."

"It's my house, right, Jacob? I mean, it's a jail, but it's *my* jail. You can't have control over every single thing I do."

Kids were laughing, leaving the house in singles and

pairs. The more the room emptied, the more I saw: smears on the walls, stains on the expensive furniture, beer puddled in the carpets, a broken lamp that had probably been worth ten thousand dollars.

Jacob didn't even notice that I was there. And now Hugo was standing behind me.

Jacob said to Harry, "You're an ingrate."

"I have a producer now," Harry said. "I have an agent."

"You could be in an *actual* jail now," Jacob said. "You could be waiting for a lawyer to take your case. Hoping he was good enough to get you out on bail."

"That's crazy," said Harry. "I didn't do anything wrong."

But his face belied what he was saying. His eyes were huge. A tall blond girl walked by, patted his butt, and said in French, "Good party, Harrison. See you very soon, *chéri*."

Jacob said to Harry, "Do you understand that I had a life of my own six months ago? I had friends and family and a community of respectable people who held me in high regard."

"Oh," said Harry.

Jacob went on, "I volunteered to guide you children, take care of you and protect you. To make sure you got a fair chance at success. I saved your ungrateful butt just this week, Harry. I asked the board not to cut years off your inheritance. I had to *beg*."

"I'm sorry, Uncle Jacob."

"Are you, Harry? Because last week, a friend of yours *died*. Then you were taken to the hospital because of a weak heart. Now you are taking substances and bringing strangers here while your siblings are in their beds. You are also disgracing the memory of your grandmother."

"I'm a wretched person, Jake. But I meant no harm."

The parlor was finally empty. Jacob closed the door and locked it.

"I was never popular," Harry said. "Now people want to be with me. I recorded my own composition and it aired in *Paris*. It was a big thing for me, Uncle Jake. How could I say no to people who wanted to celebrate with me?"

"Learn to say no to self-destructive compulsions," Jacob said. "Be smart, Harry. Make the best of your privileged situation, because in two years, I won't be your guardian. You will be free to stand on your own feet, or fall down. That will be up to you.

"But not today. In a few hours, you *will* go to school and you *will* be on time."

Harry said, "I'm sorry, Uncle Jake. I really am."

He plucked his shirt from where it hung on a lamp finial, then passed me and Hugo as he headed up the stairs.

I followed him, whispering at him fiercely, "I know you took some of those pills. Why are you lying to me, Harry? I know you. I know you as well as I know myself."

He didn't deny it. But then, he didn't say anything.

God, oh God, I don't want my brother to die.

5
TRICKS OF FATE

46

Jacob said exactly six words to me as he steered me out of the house the next morning.

"No school today, Tandy. Road trip."

I asked why, but his body language told me he was in a galaxy far, far away and didn't even hear me.

We got into Jacob's tidy white Fiat, and within a couple of minutes we were tearing south through Paris at warp speed. I grabbed on to the armrest on one side and the console on the other and held on *tight*.

What the hell was this road trip? Where were we going? Could I even trust that I was *safe*?

I kept my eyes straight ahead, feeling every intersection

as a potential collision site, watching for black cars, maybe a bunch of them barricading the road.

Jacob drove like a robot until we hit the outskirts of Paris. Finally, braking the car at a stoplight, he turned to me with a superintense look.

"You want answers, Tandy? You're going to get answers."

"What kind of answers?"

"The kind you like. Complicated."

Well, thanks for clearing that up, Jacob.

The light changed, and we were off again. I read Jacob's mood as fiercely *determined*, like whatever we were driving toward was against his better judgment. That scared me a ton.

I juggled hypothetical scenarios as we sped through Fontainebleau, and then the landscape changed and we hit the really rural vineyard area of Thomery. Jacob took dust-raising corners on two wheels and never consulted the GPS.

Suddenly, he veered onto the verge of a country road and stopped the car outside an isolated hobbit house made of brick and wood, with a roof that sagged in the middle. In front of the house was a crazy-wild garden that hadn't been tended in years.

The whole place looked like a girl who had crashed

after a wicked party and woken up with smeared makeup and her hair sticking out every which way.

Who lived in this tumbledown house? And why had we come here? I asked the boss, putting a little anger into it.

"Be patient, Tandy. You'll know shortly. But I'll tell you this right now. I used up a lot of personal favors to find these people. It's taken me years."

What people? Why had he looked for them?

I got out of the car and followed Jacob's regimental walk up a dirt path through tall weeds to a bare wooden front door.

He knocked. He knocked again, and then the door creaked open on rusted hinges. I held my breath, wondering if the person who opened it would be an enemy. Had I been led into a trap?

Two old people stood in the doorway.

The gentleman's face was heavily lined. He had a wide nose, cracked hands, a thatch of gray hair, and a bent back. His clothes were simple denim work clothes and looked like they'd been laundered a thousand times.

Standing right in front of him was a small woman about the same age, same general work-worn appearance. She wore a man's long-sleeved work shirt over baggy gray pants. Her gray hair was short and roughly cut, and her eyes were gray, too, and unflinching.

The elderly man said, "*Bonjour*, Jacob." Then he dropped his gaze to look at me.

The woman, who I assumed was his wife, fixed her gaze on me and said, "*Vous êtes la soeur de Katherine, n'est-ce pas?*"

47

When the old woman asked me if I was Katherine's sister, it was as if a whirling, sucking vortex had opened on the doorstep. There was no escape. I plunged down into this well of nauseating fear I couldn't name.

I steadied myself against the door frame and managed to say weakly, "*Oui*, Katherine was my sister."

Jacob introduced me to Étienne and Emmanuelle Cordeaux, and I kept flashing on what he'd said to me at the stoplight: *You want answers, Tandy? You're going to get answers. The kind you like. Complicated.*

The sickening feeling of dread was tied to that. Like I was about to learn what had happened to Katherine, or maybe the truth about my whole family—and I wasn't going to like it.

The old couple showed us into a teeny sitting room with a low-beamed ceiling, a couple of ancient chairs, and a sofa covered with a horse blanket. A big old shaggy dog slept in front of the wood-burning fireplace.

While Madame Cordeaux fixed tea, about a hundred questions lit up in my mind.

The top three: How did these people know Katherine? Why had Jacob taken years and used favors to get to the Cordeaux? And third, how was I going to sit through small talk without jumping out of my seat and demanding explanations—right *now*?

As I looked around the room, a tableau on the mantel reached out and grabbed my attention. There were three gilt-framed pictures of a boy about ten, long-limbed, smiling mischievously. A kid with joie de vivre and a sense of humor.

In the first photo, he romped with a shaggy, long-legged puppy. In another, he was laughing as his father carried him on his back. In the third picture, he was wearing a stiff little suit, standing on a stage, shaking the hand of an older man, who was giving him a trophy.

"Our sons," Étienne Cordeaux said in French. "Christian, Laurence, Charles. They would be twenty-four years old now."

Did he say *sons*, plural? Was this boy in fact three boys? And they were all *dead*?

Madame Cordeaux returned from the kitchen with a tray, and as she poured tea, she said, "Yes, triplets. My three beautiful, identical sons. They were good children. We thought they would work in the vineyard, have families one day..."

Monsieur Cordeaux said, "But then we were *discovered*, or perhaps you know this, Mademoiselle Tandoori."

"No. I don't. This is all news to me."

Jacob said, "It's okay to tell her, Étienne. She wants to know it all."

48

The old gentleman paused as he organized how and what he was going to tell me. I could almost see him thinking and see what he was feeling, too. His features crumpled.

At last he said, "When Emmanuelle and I were young, we worked in the lavender fields for a lady in Paris. Madame Hilda Angel. Very kind. Ten years ago, a man from Angel Pharmaceuticals came here. He brought Katherine with him. She was a striking girl in every way."

Madame Cordeaux said, *"Pardonnez-moi.* Come, Bernard." The dog got to its feet and followed her into the front garden.

Monsieur Cordeaux said, "Emmanuelle...cannot bear to talk about the boys."

When the door had closed, I used the interruption to ask, "Who was the man with Katherine?"

I was scared to hear the answer. Had it been my father? Or Jacob? Was that how he knew the way to this house by heart?

"He was Madame Hilda's son Peter Angel," said Monsieur Cordeaux. "I didn't like him very much, but I was instantly drawn to Katherine, who was about the same age as our sons.

"But Katherine was very different from my boys or any child I had ever met. She spoke several languages. She picked up the front end of my truck. She explained the genetic makeup of a virus affecting our grapes. She sang— now, there was an angel's voice. And then she went off with the boys to play.

"While they were gone, Monsieur Angel told me of an extraordinary opportunity for our boys, saying they could have better lives than we could give them. He said he would supply the pills—'harmless herbal supplements' that could raise the boys' intelligence and other things I don't even want to remember."

But Monsieur Cordeaux couldn't forget. He stopped speaking and lowered his head. Jacob looked as stricken as Monsieur Cordeaux, and I felt that vortex sucking me down again. What had those harmless supplements done to the Cordeaux children? And were they the so-called vitamins my sibs and I had been given?

Monsieur Cordeaux began to speak again. He said that Peter offered money for the children's education and that he and Emmanuelle had agreed to put their boys in the program. With Peter's own niece taking the pills, they were obviously safe.

"They did become smarter," Monsieur Cordeaux told me. "They each had a different regimen of pills, and they each became superior in a different way. The day Laurence picked up a young horse, *mon dieu*. We were... astonished.

"But then they began to age rapidly, even after we stopped giving them pills."

Monsieur Cordeaux looked at the pictures on the mantel, then got up and straightened the little shrine to his sons' memory. Jacob asked him if he could continue, and the bereaved father nodded and returned to his chair.

"There was nothing to do for them, Mademoiselle Tandoori. They withered. And after long illnesses, they died. Our pleas to the Angel company went unanswered. We are poor people, and they simply shut us out. Our feeble lawsuits died as our boys had died.

"Our boys had been perfect just as they were," he said.

"We blame ourselves for ever believing that man. Your uncle. He took everything we loved."

He looked up with his sad, tear-reddened eyes and showed me the palms of his empty hands.

"He left us with nothing."

49

We had been with Monsieur and Madame Cordeaux for only an hour, but because the visit had come with long and twisted strings attached to two families, it seemed that I had known them for years.

· I felt the most sickening shame and grief, for Emmanuelle and Étienne Cordeaux and for the deaths of their three innocent children. I couldn't hide from the devastating knowledge that Peter had found this family and seduced the parents with money and my sister Katherine's charm.

And I couldn't help also worrying that my brothers and I had been permanently harmed by the pills.

As we drove back to Paris, Jacob explained that he had begun looking into our family years ago, to find out who his long-lost brothers were. Much of what he had learned was so disturbing, he had kept his distance until recently.

I asked Jacob, "Did Malcolm and Maud know about those boys?"

"I don't know about Maud, Tandy," he said. "Malcolm had access to all the data at Angel Pharmaceuticals. From what I've learned over the years, the Cordeaux boys weren't the only guinea pigs. I've met other families, even a few survivors."

"And?"

"Some seemed to thrive. You and your siblings, for instance. Others, as Étienne said, aged fast. They died. I have theories, but no actual proof of who knew and did what. Not yet."

More shame washed over me. Tears rolled down my face, and I was so bereft, I didn't lift a finger to wipe them away. I'd mistrusted Jacob, and I'd been wrong. It was absolutely clear that he really was *trying* to protect us.

I found a tissue in my pocket. I took a moment, and then I asked, "Were all the experiments on children?"

"Yes. A lot of the kids were multiples."

Sure. In an experiment, you have a guinea pig and a control subject to compare it with. If I got the pills, maybe Harry only got placebos. Was that why my twin brother was not athletic, not intellectual, actually nothing like me or Hugo or Matty or Katherine?

Has Harry been taking placebos all along?

Was this the real reason our parents had never had any interest in him?

"The boxes in the basement," I said.

"I put them there for safekeeping. I hired the detective to follow Katherine. He took those photos of her in Paris. I was trying to watch out for her, Tandy, but I failed. God help me. I failed."

Jacob and I were both depressed beyond words when we got back to Gram Hilda's house.

Harry was in the big, spotless kitchen with its painter's view of the rose garden. He was making a big, meaty sandwich for himself, and I was struck by how young he looked, how shiny and untouched by anything gross or ugly or bad.

"Heyyyyy," he called out to Jacob and me. "Guess who's performing live tonight? Guess. Never mind. It's *me*."

50

I was in Harry's bedroom watching him freak out. He was hyper and totally unfocused. In short, he was a red-hot mess.

He was going through drawers, tossing garments over his shoulder, saying, "Michael—my agent—"

"Tall guy. Dreads. I met him, remember?"

"Okay, yeah. Michael called me like a minute before you walked in the door. He sounded weird."

Harry found a pair of tight black jeans. He hopped around getting them on while I waited to hear what was *weird*.

"He'd been negotiating but told me not to hope too much, you know? And then everything went out of control really fast..."

Harry pulled on a vintage I HEART NEW YORK T-shirt over the jeans. He jerked open his closet doors and grabbed a jacket, an iridescent coat of many colors. He put it on; it was an interesting look, both gaudy and very cool, and the colors reminded me totally of Harry's shimmery paintings.

But I was still in the dark.

"*What*, Harry? What went out of control?"

"Everything," he said.

"Say something that has a fact in it somewhere."

He laughed. "I told you. I'm going to perform *live*. *Tonight*. How's my hair? Do you like it doing its own thing?" He roughed it up with both hands. "Or do you think this makes me look older?"

He grabbed a fistful of his longish curly hair and held it in a bunch at the back of his neck.

"Harry. Look at me," I said. "You're performing *where* tonight?"

He slowly and nicely said, "The Palais Omnisports de Paris-Bercy. Oh, man, Tandy. I'm opening for Adele."

Oh. *Wow*. I was getting it. I was finally *getting* it. This wasn't like playing a gig in a bar, or in a small club. This was the BIG time. *Huge*.

Bercy, as it's called, is a gigantic sports arena that can hold almost seventeen thousand people. I'd seen videos of rock stars giving concerts there to adoring, out-of-their-minds crowds.

Harry was going to be at the center of *that*.

I screamed. Harry screamed. We grabbed each other and danced around the room. I wished C.P. was here to scream and dance with us. She would have been so proud of Harry. She would have pierced our eardrums with her screaming. But even without C.P.'s shrill vocal contribution, Harry and I made enough ruckus to bring Jacob into the room in a hurry.

I saw his face. It was like, "What now?"

Poor guy, but he was funny without meaning to be. Harry and I laughed until we were rolling on the floor.

"What's the joke?" our uncle asked.

We told him Harry's news, and after Jacob shouted, "This is *tremendous* news, Harry!" he joined us in dancing around.

Oh my God. My brother was going to be onstage in one of the most important venues on the *continent*.

My shy, overlooked brother, Harry.

51

Hugo, Jacob, and I were right there at the vast, magnificent arena known as Bercy, sitting under the pinpointed glare of lights and surrounded by the seventeen thousand people who were flowing into the enormous stadium. Our best-in-the-house seats were midway up the lower tier, where we could see directly onto the stage.

With a cracking sound, spotlights flashed on and hit the stage, followed by a feedback squeal, and then a booming, echoing voice came over the sound system. The voice thanked and welcomed the crowd and spoke of Adele in glowing terms, whipping up the crowd, which was already high on anticipation and in a near frenzy.

Then the faceless voice blared, "It is our pleasure to

introduce the pianist Harrison Angel playing his homage to Montmartre."

Harrison Angel. My brother.

To modest applause, Harry trotted up a short flight of steps onto the floating stage in the center of the stadium floor. He seated himself between his piano and organ.

To be honest, my heart clutched for Harry. He was unknown, a warm-up act for a superstar. Sitting alone on the stage in his iridescent jacket, well, Harry looked very small. Like a dragonfly under a microscope.

Then he put his fingers on the keys.

I held my breath as his amazing and uplifting first notes were overwhelmed and smothered by the sound of shuffling feet and laughter and talking that came together as one circular, three-dimensional rolling rumble.

But sometime during the first stanza, a shushing sound replaced the noises of the crowd, as though people were saying *Shhh, I want to hear.* The whisper gained strength and lapped the stadium, and by the time Harry's third burst of arpeggios danced out over the audience, his music had captivated all the hearts and souls at Bercy.

I'd only heard "Montmartre" once before, and I'd been dazzled by its beauty. Now the sound was *ginormous* but still retained its delicacy and touching emotion. I saw rapt faces all around, tier upon tier, and when the last notes of the Fender Rhodes sounded and faded, there was silence, followed by shouts of "Encore!" and the phenomenal rhythmic cracking of applause.

Beside me, Hugo was shouting, "Holy moly, Harry. Is that you?"

Harry played another tune, a composition he'd written as we crossed the Atlantic weeks ago on the *Queen Mary 2*. His piece "The Atlantic" surged and then climaxed in a crescendo, a swelling wave that seemed to travel up and down the length of the stadium.

The crowd went mad.

And then, as the applause ebbed, Adele came out onstage, and the crowd went crazy all over again. Harry stood, and Adele put her arm around him, and when she could finally be heard, she said, "Harrison Angel, my friends. This young man is sixteen. Harry, we cannot wait to hear what you will do next."

More applause, epic rounds and rounds of it.

Before Adele finished her set, Michael Pogue arrived and gathered up our small party. We were ushered to a limo and whisked to an unmarked industrial building with a heavily guarded back door. We were cleared through in an instant and entered a long hallway throbbing with music.

We were in a nightclub—Hugo, too!

And there was Harry, standing by the bar, surrounded by a thick mob that included the men I had seen in the mix room at the Smart Blue Door.

Harry was glowing. The colors of his shimmering jacket picked up every glint of light. He looked ethereal, my angel brother.

The club filled quickly with beautiful people in amazing clothes. Adele and her entourage swept in and then, unbelievably, Beyoncé and Jay Z were there. Techno music pounded, and between the dancing and shouting over the music, I wasn't sure if Harry had even seen me.

But he had. Before he was pulled away by people who wanted to touch him, shake his hand, become part of his future, Harry came to me. He grabbed me and hugged me really tight.

He spoke over the noise, right into my ear, saying, "I love you, Tandy. And no, I'm not using the filthy drugs. This is all me. *This is what we're capable of.*"

52

I woke up coughing and swamped by heart-pounding, gut-heaving panic. I heard a low roar that meant nothing to me, but I did know that the world had gone extremely wrong and if I didn't get a grip on it soon, I was going to die.

My lungs burned, that was a clue. They burned like I'd breathed in acid. I couldn't draw in a real breath. All I could do was cough and gag. Tears poured out of my eyes, rivers of tears, and it was dark. I couldn't see anything.

But I smelled perfume. Another clue. And I remembered that I was in Gram Hilda's attic workroom, where I'd gone after we'd come home from the concert. I must have fallen asleep on the floor.

But now I was not just panicked, I was disoriented.

I couldn't see the windows in her atelier, and most definitely not the door.

I was blind.

No. It was smoke, the blackest, densest smoke imaginable, the kind that meant that the fire wasn't in my lungs. The house was burning and must have been for a while for the air to be completely opaque behind a closed door on the top floor. Now that I understood my situation, I was terrified.

We could all die.

I have to wake everyone up.

Harry's bedroom was on the floor below me. So was Jacob's.

I had a flash of clarity in which I knew certain things. That I was supposed to crawl to the door, get under the layer of smoke, where the air was cleaner and cooler. I was supposed to feel the door, and if it was hot, it meant that the fire was right outside and I had to reverse course and go—where?

I was feeling faint. I only had a few seconds before I passed out—and most of those precious seconds were gone.

Where is the door?

I felt the edges of the Persian carpet with my fingers,

and, still hacking and retching, I inched on my belly toward where the door might be. I bumped into furniture. Heavy things fell all around me. But I found the door.

Not so fast, Tandy.

The door was scorching hot, and I could hear the snapping and crackling of wood burning on the other side.

That's when I forgot what I was supposed to do. I was running out of air, out of ideas, out of motivation. Heat was radiating around me on all sides, and fire flickered in the gap under the door.

I couldn't stand or get to my knees, so I rolled toward the middle of the room. But I had no plan. I was cooked.

Death by fire is supposed to be the worst death of all. Burning nerves, tens of thousands of them, shoot excruciating pain to every minute part of the body, and you just can't die fast enough.

I thought of Joan of Arc. I thought of ships burning at sea. Skyscrapers on fire. People jumping to their deaths rather than burning.

Flames licked under the door, looking for the next thing to eat.

Gasping, feeling the scorching heat on my skin, I covered my face with my arm and thought about my brothers and Jacob and hoped to God they'd all gotten out alive.

It was too late for me.

I was praying, "Please, God, let me die quickly," when there was a loud crash as the burned door, almost consumed by the blaze, fell into the room.

Flames bounded toward me. The leaping fire was ecstatic now that it had been set free. The room was blazing. Red light licked the walls and was going for the ceiling when someone burst through the door frame, urgently calling my name.

I recognized his voice. *James.*

I couldn't call to him. I was too far away, at the end of the tunnel, turning my face to the light.

And then I was lifted up. My cheek was on his shoulder. He said, "I've got you, Tandy. We're going to be okay."

That's all I remember.

James came through for me when it mattered.

He saved my life.

53

A *shock jolted me into consciousness*. I mean, like electricity shooting straight through my brain. It was not just a heinous invasion of my private thoughts, but a terrifying buzzing sound, like a blender turning my brain to mush.

I still couldn't see.

But I knew the abrasive feel of harsh cotton sheets on my naked body. I knew the stinging smell of antiseptic in my nostrils, the squealing rattle of rolling carts outside the room, and the squeaking of rubber-soled shoes on composite flooring. I knew all of that by heart.

I was at Fern Haven.

How could James have brought me here?

A dark thought occurred, darker than a black sucking hole in the universe.

Have I ever left Fern Haven?

Had I fantasized an entire year of school and my parents' deaths and Matthew's trial and all the crimes that had closed in around us in New York, cases that I had solved?

Did I make up going to Paris?

Had I been tripping at Fern Haven for...the entire time?

I heard a sound system, Dr. Someone being paged. I grabbed for the bed rails, ready to fight to the death. Any minute now, some stiffly smiling doctor or fakey-nice nurse was going to ask me if I was ready for my next treatment.

I would yell *"No no no!"* and I would lash out with my fists.

Straps would be tightened. A gag would go in my mouth. An IV line with knockout drugs would drip into me, and then—oh, God, *the electric shock*.

I couldn't let them do that to me.

Not again.

I shouted, "James!"

How could he have left me here alone?

I felt a hand on my arm. I wrenched it away.

"Tandy. It's *me*. You're okay."

I opened my eyes. It was dark in the room. The buzzing

sound was coming from a monitor to my right, and in a chair to my left—*Jacob*. He was alive. I knew him. I hadn't made him up. Had I?

"Tandy?"

Jacob was silhouetted by the windows behind him, and by a night sky full of city lights. I said something so trite, I wish I could have taken it back and said something more clever.

"Where am I?" I said.

"The American Hospital."

So I was really in Paris?

"There was a fire," Uncle Jacob said. "But everyone is okay."

I gasped as the memory of the thick, life-snuffing smoke and searing flames came back.

And I remembered my rescuer.

"Jacob. Where is James? He saved my life."

Jacob spoke as if I hadn't mentioned James at all.

"The fire started in the kitchen. Did someone leave the stove on? I don't know. Or maybe one of our modern appliances overrode the house's very old circuitry. Hugo was so brave, Tandy. He ran upstairs to find me. Through the fire."

"And Harry?" I bit the back of my hand. I needed to hear details. I needed more than that Harry was "okay."

"Harry hadn't yet come home," Jacob said. "He was still at the club when the fire happened."

That's when I noticed the pale bandages wrapped around Jacob's forearms all the way down to his fingers.

"You're hurt!"

He shook his head and said to me, "You weren't in your room. The fire was shooting up through the stairwell, and I could hardly see. I had a last-minute thought of the attic...I got there without a second to spare. I wasn't even sure you were still breathing, Tandy. I'm not joking, but I felt your grandmother in the room with us. She showed me where you were. She showed me."

I started to cry; then I collapsed into deep, heaving sobs. Jacob had risked his life for me, and this wasn't the first time. I thanked him. He hushed me. I reached for him. He hugged me awkwardly with his bandaged arms.

"The house is gone. Burned to the ground."

I wiped my face on the cotton of my hospital gown. I put my hands to my head. My hair was just a cap of frizz. But I was coming back to myself. And I hated to say what I was thinking. But I wasn't crazy. I just *knew*.

I said, "I think we're getting close to something we're not supposed to know."

"What are you saying, Tandy?"

"This was no accidental house fire, Uncle Jacob. Someone is trying to kill us."

CONFESSION

This is hard to say... James hadn't saved me from the fire, but I know I felt him moving around the hospital room as I lay, sedated, under layers of cotton sheets.

His presence was shadowy, and he hovered around my bed in the dark. He seemed occupied with thoughts that had nothing to do with me, and he seemed happy, which only made me feel sadder and more alone.

I tried to ignore him.

He was a hallucination. But still, there he was at the edge of my vision, standing beside the window, reclining in the chair, walking to the doorway before sitting on the bed, casually putting his hand on my thigh.

James.

Speak to me.

I heard only the sounds of soft footsteps outside my room, rubber-soled shoes walking along the hospital corridor.

James?

No answer.

I spoke to this ghostly James, whoever, whatever he was.

James. Listen to me. I miss you so much. I wish there was a way I could talk to you. I would tell you about all the terrible things that have happened since we were last together, events I only half understand.

And I wish you would tell me what you've been doing and thinking and feeling.

Do you miss me? Is that why I feel your presence here in my room?

I wish you were lying beside me and that we were laughing and whispering to each other again.

The truth is, James, I would give almost everything I have to be with you.

Your true Angel,

Tandy

54

Two days after the fire, only an hour after my release from the hospital, I was in a police interrogation room, where cops were accusing me of torching my grandmother's house.

They had no evidence, of course, but they'd cooked up a variety of bogus motives for me, which, where I come from, is called a fishing expedition.

They had one suspect, me. And they wanted to hook me, reel me in, and toss me into an ice locker—*today.*

The false accusation was insane, and I was already in an angry depression.

The fire had taken my computer, consumed the last letter from James. Clothes my mother had given me were destroyed, and so were Katherine's boxes. And so was Gram Hilda's gorgeous house and everything in it. I felt as if my grandmother had died all over again.

I looked as bad as I felt.

My skin was red, flash-dried by the fire. A nurse had trimmed the frizz on my head, and I was wearing tacky clothes Jacob had bought for me that morning. Thank you, Jacob, but I looked more like a meth addict than a person who should be taken seriously.

Lieutenant Bouton was pretty and hip. She looked twenty but was probably thirty. I'd thought she would be the *good* cop. But I was wrong. She was as tough as horsemeat.

While her partner, Lieutenant LaMer, sat across from me, Bouton looked for ways to maximize my vulnerability. She slammed a folder on the table and spread the papers around in front of me. They were copies of my file from the New York City police department.

Item number one was the court documents charging me with the deaths of my parents—later *dismissed*. Item numbers two and three were morgue pictures of Malcolm and Maud lying on slabs in the medical examiner's office, bloodless and gray under a cold light.

I'd seen my parents dead in their bed, so you'd think mere pictures would have no power to hurt me. But they did. Those photos reopened old wounds, rubbed salt in them, and dug around in them, too, which brought back all the old pain, anger, deep sadness, longing, and regret.

It was all beyond excruciating. I let out a sob. Then reined myself back in.

Bouton walked behind me so that I couldn't see her face.

She said, "You hate the family of yourself, mademoiselle. You want them all dead. Your father. Your mother. This is your work, is it not? You murdered them. You tricked the police and so you got away. You can run, but how do you say, you cannot hide."

"No, no, no! Are you an idiot?" I fired back in French. "Read the later reports. Read a few words, why don't you? And now someone has tried to murder *us*. Don't you get it? *We all could have died*."

Bouton flicked the back of my neck with her fingers.

"Hey!" But I was afraid if I got out of my seat, I could give her a reason to really hurt me.

"Killer girl," said Bouton, "you should tell us how you set this fire. We will find out."

She began pushing a chair in front of her like it was a baby carriage. Jostled it and banged it down on its back legs. All this was to rattle me. Make me cry and then confess.

When I didn't react, Bouton parked the chair and sat in

it. She leaned over the table and said sweetly to me, "Why *did* you set fire to the house? The house was insured for millions, *non*?"

"I was asleep," I said for the fourth time.

"But heh, you cannot prove that. There were no witnesses to you even in your bed. You admit that, correct, Mademoiselle Angel?"

"I slept in the attic. I told you."

She attacked from another direction.

"You've been sad lately, *non*? Your lover, he *dumped* you, and so you were having a mental breakdown."

"Which would be understandable," said Lieutenant LaMer. He gave me the good-cop smile.

"I didn't set the fire," I said angrily. "I was asleep by myself. On the top floor. Where I almost *died*."

There was a knock and then a pounding on the door. LaMer opened it for another cop and our family attorney, Monsieur Delavergne, who marched in.

Delavergne said, "Either charge my client now, or I am taking her home."

Home? What home?

Five minutes later, Delavergne helped me into the backseat of our car. Morel was at the wheel, and Jacob got into the backseat with me. He opened his poor bandaged arms to me and I fell against his chest.

I know I've had days as bad as this one in my life, but at that moment, this was as bad as it got. A few months earlier, I thought I was going to have a very big life.

Now I didn't want to live at all.

Honest to God. What the hell was I going to do?

55

I had to talk to Jacob, alone. Urgently.

That night, we sat in padded chairs on the terrace outside my room at the Hotel George V. The Eiffel Tower stood gloriously lit in the distance. But this billion-dollar view of Paris meant nothing to me.

My brothers and I were under siege. I'd been incredibly naïve, and it had taken a destructive fire to snap me to attention. I was shaken and appropriately scared.

I said to Jacob, "You've been saying you want to protect us, and you know what? We *need* your protection. We weren't just targets, you know. Someone was determined to burn us alive."

"The arson investigation is still ongoing. One good thing: They're no longer looking at you."

"I don't *care* about the investigation. I was stupid. I was watching out for black cars passing by. I didn't think we were going to get murdered in our sleep. You have to be a psychopath to set fire to a house full of people."

Jacob nodded. "What are you thinking?"

"Besides the fact that I'm terrified *and* horrified? I found a notebook in the attic, Jacob. Gram Hilda's handwriting. Almost like a diary."

"You read it?"

"Cover to cover. And I understood every word. Here's the instant recap. Gram Hilda created the formulas for the original pills. An early version of them, anyway. She hoped these formulas could improve the lives of impoverished children, but her follow-up of the animal studies told her that the results were unpredictable. And by that, she meant *dangerous*."

"You're sure of this, Tandy?"

"The formulas were in her book, Uncle Jake. My dad and Peter had to have found them after Gram Hilda died."

"Possible," Jacob said. He said it a couple more times. He was listening to me intently, and he looked sad. He said, "I hate to say this about my own brother, but if the products were dangerous according to Hilda, that wouldn't have stopped Peter. Not if he saw big money at the end of the day."

"I don't think he has any limits, Uncle Jake. He experimented on children in his own *family*. He's capable of anything. Are we just going to wait for him to get us? Are we?

"Because I really can't go along with that."

56

I was awake all night long, listening to a variety of alien sounds coming from above and beneath me in the hotel, as well as street noises that got louder as morning came on.

While my brothers and Jacob slept in the suite next door, I dressed fast and left the hotel. I was living in an Alice in Wonderland world where up was down and down was sideways and converging roads were consumed in fire.

I needed to clear my head.

I walked fast on Rue Clément Marot, shifting my eyes everywhere. I was a couple of blocks from the Champs-Élysées, but I had no destination in mind. I was just moving my legs and hoping that an answer to "What should we do now?" would jump into my head.

And then it *did*.

The answer was dead simple. Paris was over. We'd gotten the best of this city, and it had nothing left for us. Not when someone was trying to kill us all, even Hugo. We had to get on a freaking plane, and I wasn't even going to ask permission from Jacob.

I dodged foot traffic and made phone calls as I walked. I got routed to phone queues. I spoke to people who had to transfer my call, and I was put on hold many times.

But I did it.

We were booked on a private plane that would depart that night for the United States. Jacob would have to transfer funds and school transcripts, and he'd also have to handle Harry, who would probably go bug-nuts.

As I detailed possible living arrangements in New York, the to-do list grew.

I was crossing a street when, without warning, someone grabbed my arm from behind.

It was a shock right through my heart. I pulled back, and as I opened my mouth to scream, I faced my attacker, expecting to see a brutish thug sent by Royal Rampling.

It was a woman, small, apparently unarmed.

When I was able to hear her, I realized that she was saying, "Tandy. Tandy, it's *me*."

I stood there in the middle of the street, looking at this

stranger with dark hair and sunglasses, wearing a dark coat with a hem down to the tops of her boots. Who was she?

I had no idea.

"*Hey!*" I shouted, jerking my arm free. "I don't know you. Leave me alone or I'll call a gendarme."

This was bravado. I half expected her to pull a gun from her pocket, that's how freaked I was. Whoever she was, I wanted nothing to do with her. I may be courageous, but I still know when to walk away and when to run.

The light changed, and dodging traffic, I ran to the other side of the avenue, fast. I felt my heart beat with violent anger in my temples.

Still, the woman called out to me and closed the gap between us.

"Tandy. It's *me*! It's *Katherine*."

57

I slammed on the brakes and whipped around, and without even thinking, I screamed, "Are you *crazy*? What kind of sick scam is this? Katherine is dead."

The woman came toward me.

"Tandy. I understand. I understand, but it's really *me*. Please. Believe me, this is no joke. It's me, Tandy. Katherine, your sister. I'm alive, I'm really alive."

My head began to swim. I got spots before my eyes. Then everything went white.

A woman's voice was calling me from what seemed to be a great distance. I heard "Tandy, Tandy, please." I realized she was right next to me, speaking into my ear.

I reached out, gripping her arm, and she said, "Whoa. There you go. Can you stand on your own, Tandy?"

I tried to reconstruct it. I was there on the street with a woman who was covered up from top to toe who said she was my sister, Katherine.

Really? Was I going crazy? My eyes burned and my head hurt and I thought I would throw up. This had to be the worst kind of hoax. As much as you might wish that a dear deceased loved one was really alive, it just didn't happen.

Katherine was dead.

But at the same time my nose was telling me that I shouldn't be afraid or even ripping mad.

Se Souvenir de Moi.

"Katherine" indicated a setback between two build-ings, a place to talk. The setback was sheltered somewhat from the street and appeared to be safe. I have no memory of walking there. I was in full-blown shock and denial. But there we were, standing together in this niche, when my alleged sister took off her glasses, then peeled off her black wig.

Unbelievable, but I saw the chestnut glints in her brown hair, same as Hugo's. She had cheekbones like Maud's. And her eyes? Light brown with gold flecks and a ring of darker brown around the irises. It was like looking at my own eyes in the mirror.

I felt as though I'd been wrenched back through time and then shot forward again. I knew that what I was seeing was real. My knees buckled. I stretched out my hand to the wall of the building and this woman—Katherine—grabbed me into a hug.

"I've got you, Tandoo. Oh my God, I've *got* you."

I still couldn't speak, but I could see her more clearly now. We were the same height, the same build. Her eyes flicked over my features and mine flicked over hers.

Oh my God. *It really was Katherine*. It was *her*.

Only then did I notice that she was no longer a teenager and looked older than when I'd last seen her. There were lines in the corners of her eyes. Had they come from squinting into the sun? Or did she look older than a woman of twenty-two should look? Oh, no. Was she aging like the other children who'd the taken the pills? No, that couldn't happen. Not now.

"You're too beautiful to be dead," I said.

Katherine laughed. It was the most glorious sound I'd ever *heard*. She said, "Wow, I don't get to laugh very much. Almost never."

I laughed, too. "Me neither."

And with that, everything I'd felt in the last few minutes broke loose in a torrent of tears. My sister was back from the *grave*, alive and well. It was miraculous. A true miracle.

Katherine was sobbing, too, and as we opened our arms to each other, we both just let it all go.

I was actually hugging my sister again.

I didn't want to stop. It was the best day I'd ever had.

58

Katherine wore a blue silk scarf around her neck. She pulled it free and handed it to me.

"Cover your hair, Tandy. Keep your eyes down, and now let's walk," she said. "Keep really close to me, and if I say run, just do it, okay?"

We weren't laughing or crying anymore, but we were walking in step as we headed for the Champs-Élysées, burying ourselves in the crowd walking north.

I said, "I have too many questions."

"Some things never change," my sister said, laughing again, squeezing me around my shoulders. My God, it felt just the same as when I'd seen her half a lifetime ago.

But I did have questions.

"Katherine, what about the accident?" I said. "The motorbike and the fuel truck in South Africa. What really happened, Kath? How did you survive?"

"Let's keep walking," said my sister. "We don't have much time. I'll tell you everything, but I'm going to skip around, okay, Tandoo?"

So many memories washed over me as I walked and talked with my sister. I was remembering the cadence of her voice, the length of her fingers, and the particular way she gestured when she talked. Kath had been my greatest booster, and I had been hers. I had mourned her and missed her for years and years, and now she was looking right at me.

I loved her so much.

She said, "First and most important, you're right to be afraid. You should be even *more* afraid. You shouldn't even be walking alone on the street, Tandy, and that goes for Harry and Hugo, too. I found you easily, and that means other people can find you, too."

I looked up and around. I saw people going to work, traffic moving steadily, nothing suspicious. But if Katherine meant to scare me—mission accomplished. When my eyes met hers, I'm sure she saw the fear lighting me up.

"Why is this happening to us?" I asked her. "I don't understand at all."

"It all starts and ends with the pills," she said. "I thought he was just after me, but I see I was wrong."

"Uncle Peter."

"Yes. He was the drug specialist in our family. He was in charge of my protocols. He kept the records. And he recruited subjects for the tests.

"Peter took me on trips and tried to make me into some kind of *pet*, Tandy. He showed me off and then, since he thought he'd made me the person I turned out to be, he tried to take total possession of me. He was getting more creepy and obsessed. And yet Malcolm and Maud refused to see it. That's why I had to run—and keep running."

"And the accident? Was there really an accident?"

"There was a terrible crash. But it was no accident."

59

Katherine's expression clouded over as she told me about that life-changing day.

"My boyfriend was driving our motorbike when we were struck from behind. I was told that I was thrown against a truck in the oncoming lane. That I bounced off the hood and hit the high grasses at the side of the road. Thank God for my helmet, right?

"I learned later that a man driving behind the truck stopped his car to avoid the collision. He saw that the roadway was going to lock up because of the accident and that an ambulance might not get through in time. So he scooped me up and drove me to a hospital.

"I was damned lucky," Katherine told me. "The fuel truck exploded and went up in flames.

"But I knew nothing of that at the time. I was unconscious for days. And when I woke up, no one knew my name and I remembered nothing.

"Weeks later, when I was ready to be discharged, the man who saved me…that darling man invited me to stay with him while I recovered from my injuries, and slowly my memories came back. And then one morning, I remembered everything. Even things I didn't *want* to remember."

Katherine looked so sad. She said, "This is the hard part, Tandy.

"When I remembered the accident, I knew I had to stay underground. I saw the man who drove his bus into the back of our motorbike. He worked for Peter.

"I can't prove any of it, but I'm telling you, the accident was a deliberate attempt to kill me. And I'm sure Peter found out that I didn't die. Someone else's remains were sent to New York and buried at my funeral.

"Peter must have arranged that to maintain the fiction of my death while he hunted for me. After all these years, I'm still being hunted."

"But why, Kath? Why does Peter want you dead?"

"Because I know all about the pills, Tandy. Peter talked

incessantly to me during those long trips. He drank and he talked. I know about the experiments on children. I met most of those poor children, and I know how they died."

I blurted, "Gram Hilda's house burned down."

"I know, Tandy. I don't doubt that Peter was behind that. He's trying to destroy the whole family because we're all living evidence of his insane experiments."

I had my hands over my mouth, but I still managed to say, "Oh God oh God oh God."

Kath said, "I think Peter has future plans for those pills. Don't be surprised if a bad phoenix rises from the ashes of Angel Pharmaceuticals."

60

I still had questions, but Kath had stopped walking, and as clotted crowds of people flowed around us, I sensed that my time with my sister was about to end.

Her hand was inside the neckline of her coat, and as I watched, she pulled out a gold chain with a pebble the size of a gumdrop hanging from it.

I gasped—because I knew. The pendant was the diamond Katherine had mined in Africa before she "died."

Katherine's cheeks were wet with tears. She said, "Duck your head, Tandy." She slipped the chain over my neck and rearranged the silk scarf.

"It's yours now, little sister," she said. "Maybe it protected me. And maybe it will protect you."

She put her hands on my shoulders and said, "I've changed my name. I don't live in France, and I hate this, Tandy, but I may never be able to see you again. That goes for Matty, Harry, and Hugo, too. It would just be too dangerous for all of us. I know this is awful, especially after today. But do you understand? We simply can't take any chances. You can't tell anyone that you saw me or that I'm still alive. *Anyone.*

"And please stop being a detective. This is too big. There's too much money involved. That's why there's no end to the danger. You can't come looking for me. Promise me you won't do that."

"*No.* For God's sake, Kath. How can you ask me to promise that? Don't disappear from my life again. We can work together. We can overcome anything or anyone—"

"Tandy, finding you and seeing you was extremely dangerous, and worth every precious moment. But now I have to go."

My feelings of frantic, panicky denial changed into a kind of sickening despair. I understood that Katherine was right, but I was already feeling the terrible loss of her.

She said, "Say, 'I promise not to look for you, Kath.'"

I nodded dumbly. And then I said, "I promise, Katherine."

We interlaced our fingers like we used to do when we

swore to keep a secret. Then she kissed me on both cheeks. I took in her fragrance deeply before she broke away from me, dashed out into the avenue, and disappeared into a taxi.

I watched the cab shoot ahead—and I felt another meltdown coming on.

Katherine had come back from the *dead*. We'd touched, cried, laughed, hugged, renewed all the loving feelings we'd had for each other.

Now she was gone.

I stood there on the street, completely devastated. It was not just like losing Katherine all over again, it was almost *worse* than if she'd never appeared.

But not quite.

Katherine had told me I was right to be scared.

And she'd given me answers.

I also had more questions. Starting with "Would my brothers and I be safe anywhere?" That answer came to me like a grenade going off in my hand.

We will never be safe as long as Peter is alive.

I walked the streets for a couple of hours, sticking to the broad avenues, keeping my eyes on everything as I processed my short time with Katherine.

She was right when she said not to tell people I had seen her. That would not only be dangerous for her, but who would believe me? I had no picture of her. I had no address. I didn't even know my sister's name.

I could almost talk myself into believing I'd imagined that Katherine was alive. I could almost believe that Katherine was a ghost.

I rubbed the rough diamond between my fingers.

Then I called Jacob.

RETURN
OF THE
ANGELS

61

We deplaned at the private airport in Teterboro, New Jersey. A sleek white limo was waiting for us on the tarmac, with a surprise inside.

Our old family friend and attorney, the sophisticated, funny, and very smart Philippe Montaigne, was in the back. Even though Philippe was also Peter's attorney, I trusted and loved him. We all did.

We shouted his name, swarming over him, competing to be heard. And as the car raced toward Manhattan, he said, "If I may just get in a few words."

We all stopped talking, but there was a whole lot of giggling.

"I have big news. Through your estate managers and

with the authority vested in me, you three have purchased a four-bedroom apartment in the San Remo Apartments. As you know, it's right on Central Park, and I'm pretty sure you're going to like it."

Like it?

The San Remo, like the Dakota, is an amazing building. The San Remo was built in 1930. It has turrets and dormers and towers, grande dame stature, and tight security. We were going to *love* it.

A half hour later, when Philippe opened the front door to our new home, I was overwhelmed with happy memories. Our old UFO chandelier was hanging in the foyer, and I hoped it was connected to the doorbell, as it had been in the past.

I could see through the foyer to the living room. Our red leather sofa was there, as were the Pork Chair and Robert, a life-sized sculpture of a man watching TV and drinking a beer. Robert had been with us forever. He was like an old friend.

Hugo asked, "Our stuff was sold, Phil. How did you get it back?"

"Well, you little ruffians are back in the money," he said. "I tracked down the purchaser, overpaid, and voilà."

"Robert! Yo," said Hugo. "Voi-freaking-là."

Hugo trotted off in search of his new room, and Harry

sat down at his white-winged piano, which we called Pegasus, and played his brilliant "Montmartre" for Philippe.

Jacob made a list and then ordered in from our favorite restaurant, Shun Lee West. I called C.P. several times, and each time, my call went to voice mail.

"C.P., it's me! We're home. All of us. Please call me. Or better yet, come over."

I gave her the address, and when the UFO chandelier tootled out the theme song from *Close Encounters of the Third Kind*, I was sure C.P. had arrived. But Matty came through the door.

Oh my God. It was so *great* to see him.

Our big brother looked fantastic—in fact, better than ever. He hugged and kissed all of us, even Philippe, who wiped his mouth with the back of his hand and said to our mountainous big brother, "Please, don't ever do that again."

We all cracked up.

I had a few sober minutes with Matty before Hugo inserted himself with football questions. Hugo continued to glue himself to his hero as we partied on exotic Chinese dishes. Then, as the festivities continued, Jacob and I carried plates into the kitchen.

"Tandy, at my request, Philippe has hired an investigator. I've used this firm before."

"An investigator? What for?"

"His name is Kenny Chang, and he is the best in the city. He's coming here in the morning with a report for us on a 'person of interest.' I gave him the assignment a week ago."

And that was all Jacob would say. I prayed it wasn't about Katherine. Her secret had to stay safely hidden.

When I went to my bedroom, I saw that the view was a lot like the one from my old room in the Dakota. I stood by myself and watched the sun slide down behind the tall trees of Central Park's Ramble.

We were home. And, of course, I had questions.

First one: Who was this "person of interest"? And what was the private detective going to tell us?

62

I was dressed in new clothes and ready to meet the private investigator at nine the next morning. I fretted. I hurried slowpokes along. And when the UFO chandelier rang out, I went to the door.

Mr. Chang was about six feet tall and had slicked-back hair. He was dressed in a good gray suit, wore pricey shoes, and had a strong handshake. Along with all that cool appearance, he had a surprisingly warm smile.

I offered coffee, which he turned down, and a few minutes later, Hugo, Harry, Uncle Jacob, Mr. Chang, and I were assembled in the living room.

Mr. Chang wasn't carrying a briefcase, and he had no notes. That was because his report was brief.

He said, "Our assignment was to locate Mr. James Rampling. We found him not far from here, enrolled and living on the campus of the Jefferson School in Clayton, New York."

I gasped, and my jaw dropped open. I was entirely shocked. There were so many layers to this statement, I couldn't grasp it at first. James was *here*? Not in a mysterious school in Europe, but here in New York?

Does he still love me?

"I want to see him," I said.

Jacob said, "You only wanted to know what happened to him, Tandy. And now you know."

"Okay, and now that I know, I want to see him."

Mr. Chang was saying, "I have a man downstairs. If you want, he can drive you to Mr. Rampling's address."

I turned to Jacob, who said, "Let's just keep some surveillance on him. That would be wise, Tandy."

I nodded. It *would* be wise. If James wanted to find me, there were ways. Jacob was right, but when had the wise thing ever won out over the reckless pursuit of the one you love?

And I did still love James. I hadn't stopped.

My brothers were asking to come along for the drive, but I wasn't having it.

"I'm going," I said, "alone. Clayton is an hour away. I'll keep my phone on and I'll be back by lunchtime."

I got my phone and my keys and then said to Mr. Chang, "I'm ready to go."

63

Against Jacob's wishes but with his permission, the driver from Private drove us north in a slick blue Lincoln Town Car. Anton was a man of about thirty, crisply turned out, almost military style. He asked me only two questions: Did I want music and did I have a preferred route?

"No music, thank you, and the fastest route there is."

I turned my face to the window and watched as we took the Henry Hudson, glided past the George Washington Bridge, crossed the Harlem River into Riverdale, and headed for the Saw Mill River Parkway.

I thought about James, and so many questions resurfaced. Why hadn't James talked to me about his decision to leave me? Was his father so powerful that we didn't even stand a chance against him?

And most important, what would James's reaction be when he saw me? Anger or love?

I wanted to be with him so much my heart hurt.

I was staring out the window, picturing my run toward James, seeing him grab me up and kiss me as he'd done only weeks ago when I met him on the Place du Carrousel after our long separation.

I was so deeply inside my head that it took me a while to realize that a black Escalade in the left lane had dropped behind us. And actually, it had been in and out of my field of vision since we'd left Central Park West.

"Anton, have you noticed that Caddy? Now it's two or three cars back."

"Yes, miss. He's been on us since we started out. I don't expect any trouble. Also, so that you know, I'm armed."

Whoa. But I wasn't reassured. In fact, I was now on high alert. I turned my head to watch the Escalade through the rear window. After about a mile, it drifted away and got off the highway at the Hawthorne exit.

I checked around for other cars that might be drafting along behind us, perhaps picking up where the Escalade had left off. I also watched for fuel trucks and anything else that looked dead wrong on the Saw Mill.

I saw nothing suspicious, and then we turned off the parkway. We must be getting close.

The countryside was wooded, high-end exurban, with graceful hills and long stretches of cropped green lawns. As we approached the school, I saw a soccer field and a steepled white chapel directly ahead, and signs listing the names of some of the Jefferson School's buildings: THEATER, ARTS, MATH AND SCIENCE, LIBRARY.

As we cruised through an intersection, I saw a black Cadillac Escalade parked in front of the library. Paranoia hit me hard. Was that the same car that had been trailing us from the city?

Were we really being followed?

But no. The Caddy remained in place when we passed it.

Anton turned right off the school's main road onto a small unpaved lane flanked with grassy playing fields. A sign read BOYS' RESIDENCES, and then I saw two large white buildings that looked like dormitories. Just past the dorms were a dozen small white clapboard houses.

Anton said, "Ms. Angel, the third house on the right is James Rampling's address."

My pulse pounded in my ears.

I pulled my makeup kit out of my bag, and as the Town Car slowed, I slicked on lip gloss and fluffed my newly extremely short, curly hair. It looked good. Once you got used to it.

Anton braked, got out of the car, and opened the door for me. He asked, "Do you want me to come in with you, Ms. Angel?"

"No, thanks, Anton. I've got this."

He gave me his card with his phone number, telling me he'd have to move the car but he'd be close by. "Call me when you're ready to go."

I hardly heard him. I touched Katherine's diamond lying against my chest.

But all my attention was on the small house where James Rampling lived.

64

As I *struck out for the* porch of the white house, the front door opened and a blond boy about my age bounded out.

I stopped him, saying, "Hi, I'm looking for James."

"Rampling? His room's on the second floor."

The boy loped off, and I went through the door. The sitting and dining rooms to the right and left of the staircase were unoccupied, so of course, I took the stairs.

There were two open bedroom doors on the second floor and one closed door with a hand-lettered sign reading RAMPLING at eye level. I put my ear to the door. It was dead quiet inside, and I prepared myself for a letdown. What if I'd made the trip for nothing?

Come on, Tandy. Do it now.

I took a shaky breath—and knocked.

I heard soft footsteps and then the door swung open. A girl stood there. She was slim, wearing black lace panties and bra, but that wasn't the biggest shock. When I looked at her face, I almost had a heart attack.

I swear, my heart locked up and my brain froze.

With enormous, superhuman effort, I managed to say, *"C.P.?"*

She said, *"Tandy?"*

We both said, *"What are you doing here?"*

But my voice was louder, more shocked, more outraged.

My best friend was in scanties in James's room. There was only one way to interpret *that*.

"I'm back," I said. "I came to see James."

"You should probably leave before this gets awkward," said Claudia Portman, my former best friend. "You shouldn't just drop in on people, you know."

"Screw you," I spat at her. "What the hell are you doing with James?"

"Geez, Tandy. I've got to spell this out for you? I was writing to him, you know, as a friend, and we fell in love. Sorry."

She didn't look sorry. She looked triumphant. She looked like someone who had robbed a bank and gotten away clean. She looked like a fanged, first-class, made-for-daytime-TV bitch.

"Fuck you, C.P."

"Well, fuck you, too, Tandy."

I have to admit it. Fury burned through me like a flash fire, and I lost control over myself. I pulled back my hand and slapped C.P. hard across the face. Her skin went pink around my fingerprints. She reeled and cried out, "James! She hit me."

She turned her head, and looking past her, I saw a body in the bed, sheets draped over his midsection.

The body moved, sat up.

My heart unlocked and started galloping in place. It was more like a giant jackrabbit thumping against my rib cage, desperately trying to get out. I didn't know what was going to happen next, or if I was going to be able to handle it.

"Hi, Tandy," James said, lazily getting out of bed and pulling a pair of jeans on over his naked hips. When he got to the doorway, he looked at me, flicking his eyes over my hair, back to my fire-reddened skin.

He said, "Whoa. What happened to you?"

"Tell her, James," said C.P. "Tell her she's not welcome here."

James stepped between us, before I had a chance to smack C.P. again.

65

James stood between C.P. and me, using his outstretched arms to keep us apart.

He looked like the boy I loved entirely. And at the same time, he was so unbelievably detached I didn't recognize him at all. He was the perfect stranger: handsome, cool, unknowable.

And this did not compute. It was like finding a sign on your closet door reading FOURTH DIMENSION. ENTER HERE.

"You okay, C.P.?" he asked.

Was *C.P.* okay? *I* was the one who'd been betrayed. *I* was the one who'd been wronged. And so I just lost it—again.

"You owe me an explanation, James. Because I don't get any of this, at all."

He grunted, "Hunh." Then said, "What do you want, Tandy? Romance or the truth?"

That stung. Much worse than a slap across the face.

James clearly meant that romance and the truth were at opposite poles. That our relationship was a pretty story but a lie. And that the truth was going to crush me.

C.P. smirked, then stepped away from the doorway. She was out of my direct view, but I saw her put on James's shirt. Like she owned him.

I shouted at James, "What do you know about the *truth*? You lied to me from the start. You came to Paris to see me. Why did you tell me you *loved* me? Why would you *do* that? Why did you lead me on?"

James looked uncomfortable, maybe even flustered.

He said, "You might be crediting me with more forethought than I have, Tandy. I was glad to see you. I was with you when I was with you. And I do care about you. That's all true.

"You don't know how powerful my father is. He said he'd hurt you and the rest of your family. I believe what my father says. You should, too. And by the way, your uncle Peter is a hundred times worse than my father."

I listened intently, but nothing James said connected

with the feelings I'd thought we had shared. What he seemed to be telling me was that he was done. That I was dispensable. Disposable.

That I was history.

That should have been enough answer for me, but I had to ask the most wrenching question of all.

"How could you hook up with C.P.? She was my best friend."

James turned to watch C.P. put on a pair of jeans, then turned back and said softly, "What we had was good, Tandy. Right? So why does it have to be more than that?"

C.P. came out of the shadows and stood behind James. She looped an arm around his waist, pressed her cheek to his shoulder. I couldn't stand it anymore.

I spat, "C.P., you're *dead* to me. James, obviously, I don't ever want to see you again."

Then James said the strangest, nastiest thing of all. "Try to understand, Tandy. I have to live at a certain level. My father was going to cut me off and disinherit me if I didn't stop seeing you."

I understood. He chose money over me. What could possibly be colder or clearer than that?

I turned away from them and walked down the stairs with some of my dignity intact. No tears. No tears at all.

At least those two didn't see me cry. My parents' training had finally come in handy.

I strong-armed the front door and marched down the steps to the narrow little road. And although I didn't turn around, I was pretty sure James and C.P. were watching me through the upstairs dormer window.

But the car wasn't there.

About then, I remembered to phone Anton. It took a few minutes for the Lincoln to round the corner, but then it was coming for me like a great blue chariot sent by the forces of good.

Anton opened the door and I got in.

"Please take me home, Anton," I said.

"You bet, Ms. Angel."

I looked at my phone. I'd been inside that house for a total of twelve soul-searing minutes. But as horrific as those minutes had been, it was a cure for that lying, cheating snake, James Rampling.

Who, by the way, was nothing to me.

66

My mind was resolved, but my heart was shredded.

I put my hands over my face and wept, and I didn't even care that Anton could hear me. I pretended the car was driving itself and wrapped myself in my shattered illusions.

How had I been so blinded by James? How had C.P. been able to betray me with no remorse at all? How could I ever trust anyone again, ever?

The parkway wound through a wide cut in a woodland. As the leafy miles breezed by, I dried my eyes and gathered my strength. I began to analyze both the facts and the holes in the story in the hope that I would arrive at some giant breakthrough.

To start with, Royal Rampling and Peter Angel were our sworn enemies.

Rampling's motive was revenge. He'd lost a fifty-million-dollar fortune by investing in Angel Pharma before it went bankrupt. He was vindictive and had proven that he'd do whatever it took to keep me away from his son. He had hurt me. But he hadn't murdered anyone.

James was right when he said Peter was more evil than his father. Peter's motive was financial, and he had no conscience. He had hurt people for sure, been responsible for the deaths of *children*, and he was desperate to eliminate the remains of his experiments, good, bad, and ugly.

Katherine had said not to be surprised if a bad phoenix arose from the ashes of Angel Pharma, and I wondered if Peter and Royal Rampling could be in a partnership to bring the company back. Reinvent it. Recover the lost millions.

And then I had my big idea.

Every time an Angel sneezed, the press assembled.

What if we gave the press the whole story? That children had been dosed with untested pills to give them superpowers. *But wait—there's more.* Many subjects aged fast and died young. Yes. The pills were often lethal. I could see the media going crazy over this irresistible tale of greed, cruelty, and murder.

It might not all be provable, but the press didn't depend on the facts. If the scandal was big enough, Peter Angel would stay far away from his family. Rampling would stay away from us, too.

Or—on the other hand...

The absolute opposite could happen. There could be a mad rush to put Angel Pharmaceuticals in business again. There would be a big demand for superpills for superkids. Going public could be the best thing that ever happened to Peter.

I was thinking about Angel Pharmaceuticals, the Next Generation, when a black car filled the window to my left, blocking out the light.

Before I could tell what was happening, the SUV scraped long and hard against the body of our Town Car. Metal screamed against metal. Sparks flew.

My God. We were being attacked.

67

The black Cadillac Escalade had the same license plate as the one I'd seen off and on all day. It was grinding the side of our car, maneuvering us toward a steep, rocky drop-off to the reservoir far below.

I was too scared to scream.

Anton seemed to be coping well with the attack: braking, evading, racing ahead. I looked to see who was driving the Escalade but couldn't see through its tinted glass. Then there was another shock as the SUV slammed against our side panels, even as Anton buzzed down his window. He had his gun in his hand, a semiautomatic, and he was firing at the Escalade's right front tire.

He yelled to me, "Miss. Get down on the floor."

I wrestled with my seat belt, then dropped to the floor of the car and crouched there.

Shots rang out, but I could tell that the Escalade hadn't been stopped because we were now being rammed from behind, followed by more awful scraping against the left side of our vehicle.

I popped up to get a fix on what was happening, and for sure, the Escalade was still pushing us hard toward the thin metal guardrail that stood between the Town Car and the immense void at the bottom of the cliff.

More shots pinged, and this time *we* were taking fire. Glass shattered, and Anton barked out a yell; then he groaned and slumped to the side.

The car veered in a gentle arc toward the guardrail, and at the same time a voice on the car radio asked Anton to respond. Which he didn't do.

I called out to him, then leaned over the front seat. What I saw was worse than I could have imagined.

Anton had been shot through the temple. He wasn't breathing or moving—I knew he was dead. Anton had lost his life protecting me. I couldn't help him—and now I was alone.

If I didn't somehow get control of this driverless car, I was living the last minutes of my life.

There was only one thing to do. I reached over the

back of the front seat and grabbed the steering wheel. I wrenched it to the left and brought the vehicle back to the roadway just as the drop-off ended and was replaced by a wall of rock.

But the Escalade was coming up fast on my left again. At the same time, because I couldn't give it any gas, the Town Car was slowing down. I desperately wanted to get to the wooded area a hundred yards ahead, somehow engineer a soft crash landing in the trees, then jump out and hide.

Meanwhile, the Town Car was grinding against the rocky outcropping. As the friction of metal against rock slowed the car to a violent stop, I looked for Anton's gun and saw it on the floor under the gas pedal.

I was readying myself to climb over Anton's body when I heard a loud engine roar. I glanced over my shoulder.

Another car was coming up from behind, heading toward the Town Car at high speed.

I was outnumbered. I was done.

68

Anton was dead. And I was next.

I scrunched down on the floor of the back compartment and covered my head.

My mind swirled with fear, and thoughts about my too-short life were broken up with bright flashes of relief that soon I could put down the despair and anguish I'd been carrying for too long.

Just then, there was a new sound, the *rat-a-tat-tat* of automatic gunfire, followed by the *whoosh* of a speeding vehicle flying past the Town Car.

I knew I should stay down, but I couldn't do it. I just couldn't. I poked my head up and saw that the car that had been speeding toward my Town Car had passed by and was going after the Escalade.

Time stretched like a rubber band. The sound of each rapidly fired bullet was distinct. I saw each of the Escalade's tires blow out, and each blowout propelled the SUV farther into a screeching wild spin, until it flew off the asphalt and into the thicket of mature trees at the edge of the parkway.

There was a horrific crash that seemed to unfold one long second at a time. Smoke billowed, and even from so far away, I could smell burning rubber.

Then the band snapped back and real time resumed.

The pursuit vehicle pulled alongside the Escalade and braked. The driver got out of his car, but his vehicle blocked my view of him. He seemed to inspect the crashed Escalade, then get back into his car. Immediately, he began to back up at high speed toward the Town Car.

I ducked again. A hit man was coming for *me*. I was going to be executed gangster-style. Why? And by whom?

As if that mattered anymore. This was the end.

There was a tapping on the window above my head. A voice called, "Ms. Angel. Tandy! Are you all right?"

The rear door of the Town Car opened, and I peeked up to see Mr. Kenny Chang. He looked scared—for me.

A river of relief ran through me.

I recovered from the shock enough to say, "Mr. Chang. I think Anton is dead."

Chang said, "There are two fatalities in the Escalade. I'll call the authorities. Actually"—we both heard sirens at the same time—"I'm sure the state police are already on the way."

"Who died?" I asked. Was it James and C.P.? Finishing out his father's orders to get rid of me?

"Let's wait for a positive identification."

"I have to know now."

My legs were wobbly, but I was sure I could reach the smoking one-car wreck that had smashed spectacularly into the thick stand of trees.

"Tandy, it's an ugly scene," said Mr. Chang. "Trust me. It's something you really don't want to see."

I started walking.

Mr. Chang called out, "Tandy. No walking on the highway, okay? I'll drive you there."

It was a short ride, maybe a hundred yards. When Chang's car was alongside the wreck of the Escalade, I got out of the car and peered into the crumpled front seat, where two bleeding, twisted bodies lay half covered by airbags.

I looked closer at their faces, and what I saw made me scream.

Then I collapsed. Just freaking passed right out. I heard Mr. Chang calling my name, but honestly, I didn't want to wake up again. Ever.

CONFESSION

There's more I have to tell you, of course. So much more. Let me start with this: I've checked into an institution in Upper Manhattan. Waterside is something like Fern Haven, but the doctors here are trying to help me, not experiment on me, and going for treatment was *my* idea.

Still, Waterside is kind of a madhouse. There is no cone of silence here. I hear screams of people enduring detox, doctors being paged at all hours, sirens, and all the noise that is the backdrop of the city that never sleeps.

At Jacob's insistence, Private has stationed a twenty-four-hour rotation of armed guards, and someone is always right outside my room.

Sometimes I feel safe.

But the gory death tableau in the Escalade haunts me night and day. At first, it was hard to identify the crushed bodies, but finally, I recognized the driver. He was one of Royal Rampling's goons, who had boiled out of that SUV on the Place du Carrousel in an attempt to separate James and me.

The dead man in the passenger seat was Royal Rampling, none other. He had personally fired on the Town Car, had personally tried to shoot me. And now he was gone for good.

But Peter Angel is still alive, and he could be anywhere. He is still a threat to me and everyone I love. Sometimes, when I sleep, it feels as if he's a gargoyle perched on my headboard, leering as I dream.

As for my treatment, I've been diagnosed with "extreme exhaustion," or as the admitting physician said to me, "You've undergone more stress in the last few months than most people experience in a lifetime. You need a break, Tandy."

But I wasn't going to get it yet.

Day one, while I was still shaking from stress, I got a note in the form of a greeting card: flowers on the outside, some words printed on the inside, *Thinking of you*.

Then there was a message. I could hardly keep my eyes on the tangle of words in a handwriting I recognized.

Dear Tandy,
I feel horrible. I know I was wrong to hook up with James and I was weak and there is no excuse and I don't even know

*how to convincingly say "I'm sorry." But I really, truly am. I
was lonely. I missed Harry. I missed you. And then James was
right here.*

You know how he is, Tandy.

I really had no power to refuse him.

*It's not an excuse. It's just a poor explanation. But maybe
this will make you feel better. Right after you left the resi-
dence hall, James told me to go.*

He dumped me, Tandy. On my ass. And you know why?

Because he's still in love with you.

Reading C.P.'s words hurt in so many ways, I couldn't begin to
list them.

I skimmed the rest of C.P.'s note in one painful flash. She wrote
that she wanted to visit me and that she would make everything
up to me and that she would work hard to prove to me that we
could be friends again.

By the time I got to the *X*s and *O*s, I was ripping mad, crazy
mad, feeling a rage like I'd never felt before. Maybe it was not
just anger at C.P. and at James, but unexpressed fury at my
parents and my uncle Peter all rolled up into this one rotten
thing.

I'd been savagely betrayed by so many people I had loved.

I was even furious at *myself* for ever loving any of them.

I crumpled C.P.'s disgusting card; then I straightened it out so that I could shred it into tiny pieces. When all that was left of C.P.'s spidery apology was a pile of confetti, I scooped it into my fist and then flushed every word down the toilet.

I felt relieved.

But I was still a mess.

69

My therapist at Waterside is Dr. Mary Robosson.

I actually like her quite a bit. We're dealing with some heavy stuff, mostly trying to peel back the thousands of rubbery layers of lies I've been told to find the truth about my life.

We're also talking about love and what it means. This is going to be a long course, and I'm not looking for short-cuts. I have a lot to learn about love, when it's real and when it's not. Dr. Robosson assures me I will love again.

"Really?"

"Definitely. You're just sixteen. First love isn't last love or only love or even the best love. The pain you feel is appro-priate. You've been hurt, and not because of something you did or didn't do, Tandy. You're very real. And you're wonderful."

I won't lie. I have thought about both C.P. and James a lot, even after I thought I'd wiped them out of my mind. I confess that I've written them each a few letters under the heading of "people who are dead to me," but I've deleted all the letters without sending.

That's a pretty effective kind of therapy. James and C.P. matter less and less to me as the pain drains away.

I spend more time remembering the Cordeaux family in France: how their lives were savaged by Peter. I think about Monsieur Laurier at the Parfumerie Bellaire and his long-lasting love for Gram Hilda. I'm very grateful for her incredible generosity, and I think about her lovely house, which was our home when we didn't have any other.

It's gone, and yet I remember every room and every view, the whole length and breadth and depth of it. In a way, the Gram Hilda museum is now within me.

I still meditate about the things *I've* done wrong, as Father Jean-Jacques had prescribed. It helps me feel acceptance about the people who have hurt me, because we all have reasons for the things we do, whether justified or not. And one of those reasons might actually be *love*.

Case in point: Malcolm and Maud left me damaged, I know, but they loved me. And so I can forgive them.

Jacob, Harry, and Hugo visit almost every day. Even Matty comes to visit as often as he can. Hugo wears a T-shirt that reads WHAT DOESN'T KILL YOU MAKES YOU STRONGER.

He strikes poses, like he's a bodybuilder, and that makes me laugh. Every time.

It's indisputable that my family and I have been tried, tested, even baptized by fire, and we share the strongest possible bonds siblings could have. And that includes my sister, Katherine...the Angel who rose from the dead.

CONFESSION

Yesterday, I got an e-mail from an address I didn't recognize. I was about to delete it, but for some reason—boredom, curiosity, gut instinct—I clicked it open.

The subject line read, "Someone I want you to meet."

The body of the e-mail contained only a link to a video—but not so fast. *Who*, exactly, wanted me to meet *whom*? Was this hate mail from Peter? Had Mr. Rampling sent another threat in the form of a virus, this time from the grave? Was C.P. trying to reach me again?

For better or for worse, I was curious. And so, with great trepidation, I clicked on the link.

The video opened on a close-up of a darling baby in a carrier. He was wearing blue, and between giggles, he beat the air with his little hands and cooed. At the halfway mark of the twenty-second clip, another face came on the screen.

It was Katherine.

She said, "Tandoo, meet your nephew, George. He's the sweetest little boy in the world and also very, very special. I'm going to tell him all about you."

The baby was gorgeous, and he had Katherine's eyes. *My* eyes.

Katherine looked at me through my computer screen and breathed, "I love you." She grinned and kissed the baby's hand. They both waved—and the screen went black.

Tears shot out of my eyes.

I played the video over and over again, each time feeling elated, connected, renewed, and yes, *curious.*

Kath had said that George was very special. In what way? I was aching to see him, to hold him, and to know more. And I haven't told this to anyone before now.

I swear I *will* see Katherine again if it's the last thing I ever do. That's part of my plan for the future.

And when I have more to tell, I promise I'll confess all.

Your sadder, smarter, and cautiously hopeful friend,

Tandoori Angel

Chapter 1

Whit

THERE'S BLOOD EVERYWHERE. Bright red pools of it on the gurney, and still there's more gushing out, running in rivulets to the floor. It seems impossible that there could be a single drop left inside the little girl. Her face is obscured by a tangle of dark hair, but the skin I can see has gone gray and her breath comes in harsh, wet gasps.

I rush to her side as the rookie attendant who brought her in retches in the corner. "Stabbed," he heaves, barely getting out the words. "Multiple times."

"Who—" I begin.

"The Family," he spits.

I rip away the girl's shirt to reveal the worst of the damage as Janine, a newly trained trauma nurse at City Hospital, presses her fingers to the thin little wrist.

"There's no peripheral pulse," Janine barks. "We've got to hurry."

"Tell me something I don't know," I growl. I put my

hands on the girl's punctured abdomen and begin to recite a healing spell.

Unfortunately I'm getting used to this kind of work. And I owe it to the Family, a secretive, savage cult that's been terrifying the City for weeks. Every day there's a new robbery or assault, a new reason to fear. I'm no stranger to the criminal element—hell, *I* was a wanted criminal under the New Order—but members of the Family make the average robber look like a puppy swiping a treat. They live to steal, and they don't care who they hurt. Even if it's a little kid.

The girl gives a weak cough. My fingers tingle as I feel my powers beginning to build. I picture being inside her body, following the paths of her blood, searching out the wounds and binding them back together with magic.

Janine brushes the girl's black hair away from her face, and that's when I nearly fall backward in shock. This isn't some random street kid who was in the wrong place at the wrong time.

It's Pearl Marie Neederman.

Lying near death on a cold metal table is the girl who once snatched my sister and me away from The One's zombie wolves. The kid who helped nurse Wisty back from the brink of death from the Blood Plague. The fierce little survivor who now looked more dead than alive. I let out a strangled cry. *"Pearl!"*

Janine gasps. "Oh, Whit," she cries. "Can we save her?"

It's not looking good. "I don't know," I say.

My fingers flex as they aim their healing magic, and Pearl's breath steadies. But then suddenly the electricity of the M starts to feel weird. Unbalanced. Instead of a tingle, it's a prickle, then a sting. An intense ache begins spreading from my fingertips, radiating up my arms and into my head.

"Something's wrong," Janine yells.

I don't understand what's happening, but it's *bad*. I close my eyes and try to beat back the surging pain.

A nurse appears at my elbow, screaming. "What do you think you're doing?" she yells. She tries to shove me aside so she can pack Pearl's wounds with gauze.

"Voodoo," snarls another. "The girl needs donor blood, not spells."

She's wrong. Even through my rising panic, I'm sure of it. I've been working at the hospital ever since we formed the new Council, and I've seen enough to know that magic is Pearl's only hope.

But Janine is the only one on my side. The only person in the entire room who believes in me, that what I'm doing is right.

The door bursts open and the Neederman family rushes in. Hewitt's shirt is on inside out and the look on his wife's face nearly tears my heart out.

"Oh, my baby," Mama May cries. "My little baby—"

"Those barbarians!" Hewitt spits out vehemently.

I'm giving it every ounce of strength I've got, but I'm feeling exactly what Pearl's feeling: my heart spasming, my lungs filling with blood, choking off my oxygen. My brain shooting off electric charges of terror.

I'm capable of thinking two things. The first: *I faced down the evil Mountain King to rescue this kid, and I am not going to give up now.*

And the second: *how awful it is to die.*

"Her blood's going acidic—" Janine calls.

My eyes fly open and I see Wisty blaze in and skid to a stop, her eyes sparking in fear.

"Whit," she cries. "You're *bleeding!*" She stumbles toward me and a nurse grabs her, holding her back. Wisty pushes her off, but another nurse snatches her other arm, and now they've got her pinned.

"Let her go," I gasp through intense throbbing, trying to keep focus on Pearl. *I can't let this little girl die. She's like another sister to me.*

The staff is no match for a determined Wisty, who shakes them off like gnats. Then she's at my side, yelling.

"Whit, you have to stop. It's killing you—"

Her voice sounds like it's a million miles away. When she hits me, hard, on the arm, I can barely feel it.

"*Blood!*" Wisty screams. "Blood is pouring out of your ears!"

Chapter 2

Whit

I'M BLEEDING out of my *ears*? That might explain the agonizing pain in my head, like something's inside my brain and chopping at it with an *axe*.

"More time," I gasp. My hands are sticky with gore and the spells are gone. Pearl and I are racing together to the gates of Shadowland.

Then Wisty's grabbing at my shirt, pulling me away. She's screaming my name. *No!* I want to shout. *I can't leave Pearl now. Not ever.* But Wisty's using magic now, too—on me. She yanks me back against the wall.

Pearl's eyes fly open, silver and unseeing. They roll back in her head. Then her body shudders—and goes still.

Wisty wraps her arms around me. "It's over," she whispers. "We lost her."

I slide out of Wisty's embrace and sink to the floor. "Exsanguination": bleeding to death. A terrible word for an even more terrible fate. "No, *I* lost her," I moan.

Wisty crouches down by my side. "It was too late," she says gently. "No one could have saved her. Not even you." Tears glitter in her eyes and she tries to blink them away. Behind her, I can see Mama May and Hewitt holding each other, rocking back and forth in their grief. I'm too wrecked to cry.

"Don't listen to them," Wisty urges.

I don't know what she's talking about. I'm numb. "Don't listen to who?" I say flatly.

That's when I start to hear them: all the nurses and doctors who watched the battle I lost to Death.

"Freak," one of them says.

"No one should have such unholy powers," says another.

And I realize they're talking about *me*.

Janine's voice cuts through the noise, pleading. "Please," she says. "Be reasonable—he's saved so many lives—"

But no one's listening to her. The angry clamor builds until I want to cover my ears.

"He's a *monster*."

"He might have helped kill that little girl."

I clench my fists until my nails cut gashes into my palms. Those people have no idea how much Pearl gave to me, to my family. How much she suffered, too.

"He needs to submit," says a tall, sour-faced doctor.

Wisty stiffens and her cheeks flush red. "Don't even say that word around me," she yells.

The doctor's face contorts into a cruel grimace. "*Submit*," he says again. "Give up your dark magic. Both of you."

He doesn't care that Wisty and I stopped General Matthias Bloom from surrendering our City to the wicked Mountain King. Or that we defeated The One Who Is The One and ended his totalitarian reign of terror. No: all that matters to this man is how much he hates our powers.

Our powers—the phrase taunts me. How could I save an entire City but not one little girl's life?

"Abomination," says a nurse.

"Speak for yourself," Wisty says defiantly. "I didn't see any of *you* saving Pearl's life." Then she reaches out and grabs my bloodstained hands. "Get up, Whit. You need to show me you're okay."

I hear the fear in her voice, and I struggle to stand. As Wisty hurries me away, Janine catches my eye. But Mama May and Hewitt don't look at me as they clutch each other in their overwhelming grief. I will never be able to make up for this loss.

When we get outside, the sunlight feels like a slap in the face. Pearl is dead, and everyone in the hospital thinks I'm a demon. Maybe even the Needermans do, too.

The sobs come now in a wretched-sounding torrent. "How could the Family *do* that to a little girl?" I croak.

Wisty's face goes dark. "Actually," she says, and then stops and shakes her head.

"Actually what?"

"The Family didn't kill Pearl, Whit." She swallows. "She was a *member* of the Family."

I don't think I heard Wisty right. I shake my head. "No. That's impossible."

"You know there was a robbery this morning," Wisty goes on. She takes a deep breath. "And now you need to know that Pearl wasn't the victim of the crime. She was the one committing it."

I'm too stunned to speak.

"She robbed that store with a gang of kids. But unlike the rest of them, she didn't get away."

Pearl, a knife-wielding outlaw? My brain just can't comprehend it. And then, whether it's exhaustion or grief or shock, I don't know—everything goes dark.

Chapter 3

Wisty

THE ALERT COMES IN seconds after I've helped a barely conscious Whit into his bed. There's been another break-in, this one at a theater down by Industry Row.

I pull the covers up to my brother's chin. "Be safe," I whisper, "I've got to run."

Whit's proud of me for signing on as a consultant to the police force—he says I'll be *way* better at it than I was as a member of the Council—but right now he clutches my hand. Hard.

"*You* be safe," he gasps, and then slips back into his fever dream. It's a little unnerving.

A dirty kid on the street corner stares in wonder as I climb onto my chromed-out motorcycle and pull back on the throttle. His gray eyes remind me of Pearl's, and my throat constricts in a flash of pain. I hope the hospital staff lets the Needermans light a candle for her, but after that nasty scene in the operating room, I kind of doubt they will.

I peel out into the street and tear down the main thoroughfare, going way too fast. I want everything that's bad—Pearl's death, my brother's collapse, and the voices demanding that we *submit*—to get blown away by the wind.

I don't know why people have started talking about magic like it's a weapon to be confiscated. Yes, the City's suffered through more than its share of evil magic: from The One, and the Mountain King, and loathsome Pearce, just to name a few. But who, in the end, stopped the villains? People with *good* magic. People like my brother and me.

It doesn't matter to the Normals, though. Supposedly they've even developed a procedure that sucks the power out of you like a vacuum. Surrender your gift, they say, and you'll live a life of peace and quiet and contentment.

Honestly, I can't imagine anything worse.

I race down a tree-lined avenue, alongside the newly reopened art museum. A half mile past that is the almost-finished new aqueduct, still crawling with workers as busy as ants. But then I careen around a corner and have to screech to a halt, seconds before ramming into an old man carrying a squawking chicken under his arm. It's market day: the town square is jam-packed with vendors, selling everything from fruit and vegetables to resoled shoes and jerry-rigged bicycles.

I take a deep breath, downshift, and begin to weave my way through the throngs. It's proof that under the new Council, life's returning to normal. Our City is healing. The kids kidnapped by the Mountain King are back with their families, and General Bloom, that dough-faced trai-tor, is in exile.

We had to learn the hard way that adults couldn't be trusted with City leadership: power corrupted them too easily. By unanimous vote, we banned anyone over nineteen from serving on the Council.

And so far, so good. The market's hopping, and the nearby central stadium—where we can host everything from foolball matches to rock concerts to benefits for new schools and health centers—is back in business.

Take that, you middle-aged cynics!

A stray dog skitters in front of me, and I swerve to the right, knocking a basket of oranges onto the ground. I don't have time to stop, so I snap my fingers and the oranges float up, spin around, and deposit themselves back into a neat stack.

The surly vendor shoots me a black look, then makes the sign I've seen all too much of lately: two fingers crossed in an X in front of her chest, like she's warding me off. It's an ancient gesture, left over from the days when people believed in man-eating goblins and bloodthirsty bogeymen. It means, basically, *Demon, begone.*

Some people are so rude!

A guard stationed by the fountain raises his baton at me. "Walk the bike," he hollers.

I pretend not to hear him. It's not a *bicycle*—it's the fast-est machine in the entire City, and I'm definitely not going to walk it. But then he plants himself in front of me.

"Turn off the motor," he says. His eyes are narrow and mean.

"I'm in a hurry," I tell him. "Police business."

"Turn off the motor, witch."

The way he says that word makes it sound like a curse. My skin begins to tingle and flush. *No one* talks to me like that. Not today—or *any* day.

"I said turn off—" he begins.

But tongues of fire are licking out of my fingertips.

His eyes widen and he takes an involuntary step back, knocking over the same basket of oranges. The vendor curses, but she can pick up her own damn oranges this time.

"Oh dear, what's this?" I say, faking total confusion. The ends of my hair have combusted, the red curls turning into the delicious heat of curling flames. "Could I maybe just…scoot by you? *Sir?* I, uh, seem to be on *fire*…."

The guard reaches into his belt—maybe he's going to call for backup, or maybe he's going to actually try to hand-cuff me (as if!)—but I *seriously* don't have time for this. So I close my eyes in concentration, and then—*fwoop*—my bike and I have rematerialized on the other side of him. Still in neutral, I gun the engine until it roars like a mythic beast.

The guard whirls around, reaching out to grab me, but I shift into gear and pull back on the throttle. I focus my power, and, using my own magic and the motorcycle's absolutely kick-ass engine, I rocket into the sky, shooting over the final six market stalls before landing on the other side of the square, flames following me like the tail of a comet.

Over the engine, I can hear the crowd gasp in awe—or maybe horror. Then I launch a white-hot fireball high over the street, and it explodes into a shower of multicolored sparks.

Submit? Never. I live to *burn*.

Also by James Patterson

ALEX CROSS NOVELS

Along Came a Spider • Kiss the Girls • Jack and Jill •
Cat and Mouse • Pop Goes the Weasel • Roses are Red •
Violets are Blue • Four Blind Mice • The Big Bad Wolf •
London Bridges • Mary, Mary • Cross • Double Cross •
Cross Country • Alex Cross's Trial (*with Richard DiLallo*) •
I, Alex Cross • Cross Fire • Kill Alex Cross • Merry Christmas,
Alex Cross • Alex Cross, Run • Cross My Heart • Hope to Die •
Cross Justice (*to be published November 2015*)

THE WOMEN'S MURDER CLUB SERIES

1st to Die • 2nd Chance (*with Andrew Gross*) •
3rd Degree (*with Andrew Gross*) • 4th of July (*with Maxine Paetro*) •
The 5th Horseman (*with Maxine Paetro*) • The 6th Target (*with
Maxine Paetro*) • 7th Heaven (*with Maxine Paetro*) •
8th Confession (*with Maxine Paetro*) • 9th Judgement (*with
Maxine Paetro*) • 10th Anniversary (*with Maxine Paetro*) •
11th Hour (*with Maxine Paetro*) • 12th of Never (*with
Maxine Paetro*) • Unlucky 13 (*with Maxine Paetro*) •
14th Deadly Sin (*with Maxine Paetro*)

DETECTIVE MICHAEL BENNETT SERIES

Step on a Crack (*with Michael Ledwidge*) •
Run for Your Life (*with Michael Ledwidge*) •
Worst Case (*with Michael Ledwidge*) •
Tick Tock (*with Michael Ledwidge*) •
I, Michael Bennett (*with Michael Ledwidge*) •
Gone (*with Michael Ledwidge*) •
Burn (*with Michael Ledwidge*) •
Alert (*with Michael Ledwidge*)

PRIVATE NOVELS

Private (*with Maxine Paetro*) • Private London (*with Mark Pearson*) • Private Games (*with Mark Sullivan*) • Private: No. 1 Suspect (*with Maxine Paetro*) • Private Berlin (*with Mark Sullivan*) • Private Down Under (*with Michael White*) • Private L.A. (*with Mark Sullivan*) • Private India (*with Ashwin Sanghi*) • Private Vegas (*with Maxine Paetro*) • Private Sydney (*with Kathryn Fox*)

NYPD RED SERIES

NYPD Red (*with Marshall Karp*) • NYPD Red 2 (*with Marshall Karp*) • NYPD Red 3 (*with Marshall Karp*)

STAND-ALONE THRILLERS

Sail (*with Howard Roughan*) • Swimsuit (*with Maxine Paetro*) • Don't Blink (*with Howard Roughan*) • Postcard Killers (*with Liza Marklund*) • Toys (*with Neil McMahon*) • Now You See Her (*with Michael Ledwidge*) • Kill Me If You Can (*with Marshall Karp*) • Guilty Wives (*with David Ellis*) • Zoo (*with Michael Ledwidge*) • Second Honeymoon (*with Howard Roughan*) • Mistress (*with David Ellis*) • Invisible (*with David Ellis*) • Truth or Die (*with Howard Roughan*) • Murder House (*with David Ellis, to be published September 2015*)

NON-FICTION

Torn Apart (*with Hal and Cory Friedman*) • The Murder of King Tut (*with Martin Dugard*)

ROMANCE

Sundays at Tiffany's (*with Gabrielle Charbonnet*) • The Christmas Wedding (*with Richard DiLallo*) • First Love (*with Emily Raymond*)

OTHER TITLES
Miracle at Augusta (*with Peter de Jonge*)

FAMILY OF PAGE-TURNERS

MIDDLE SCHOOL BOOKS
The Worst Years of My Life (*with Chris Tebbetts*) • Get Me Out of Here! (*with Chris Tebbetts*) • My Brother Is a Big, Fat Liar (*with Lisa Papademetriou*) • How I Survived Bullies, Broccoli, and Snake Hill (*with Chris Tebbetts*) • Ultimate Showdown (*with Julia Bergen*) • Save Rafe! (*with Chris Tebbetts*) • Just My Rotten Luck (*with Chris Tebbetts, to be published October 2015*)

I FUNNY SERIES
I Funny (*with Chris Grabenstein*) •
I Even Funnier (*with Chris Grabenstein*) •
I Totally Funniest (*with Chris Grabenstein*)

TREASURE HUNTERS SERIES
Treasure Hunters (*with Chris Grabenstein*) • Danger Down the Nile (*with Chris Grabenstein*) • Secrets of the Forbidden City (*with Chris Grabenstein, to be published September 2015*)

HOUSE OF ROBOTS
House of Robots (*with Chris Grabenstein*)
Robots Go Wild! (*with Chris Grabenstein, to be published December 2015*)

KENNY WRIGHT
Kenny Wright: Superhero (*with Chris Tebbetts*)

For more information about James Patterson's novels, visit
www.jamespatterson.co.uk

Or become a fan on Facebook